GEIST ESSER

THE STORY

GEIST ESSER

THE STORY

JIM VON TESMAR

Library of Congress Control Number:		2017915064
ISBN:	Hardcover	978-1-5434-5429-1
	Softcover	978-1-5434-5430-7
	eBook	978-1-5434-5431-4

Print Information available on the last page.

Rev. date: 10/12/2017

To order additional copies of this book, contact:
Xlibris
1-888-795-4274
www.Xlibris.com
Orders@Xlibris.com
768354

DEDICATION

This book is dedicated to Charles and Elizabeth von Tesmar, my parents. Without them I would not be.

To my buddy and fellow actor, director and playwright, Larry, with whom I have worked closely on this story.

This is a story about the evil in the world. The Evil that is rampant. The Evil that seemingly rules the world. And it seems to do it so easily; almost without effort. It is as if people can't wait...

Anima (ān'ə-mə) n. The inner self of an individual; the soul.

PRELUDE

(Forty years previous)

1

Thomas Czarenovich is recently released from prison. He had been in Attica Prison in upstate New York for 14 years for rape, kidnapping, armed robbery and a few other equally nasty unlawful offenses. His rap sheet began when he was 13 years old. He started with jacking cars and robbery.

His age is 49. However, his type of living is such that some would estimate his age at nearer 60. His gray hair isn't all there anymore. His face is wrinkled like an older man would have. It does have to be said that he is dressed pretty well.

He is not a nice man and yet here he is free as a bird driving a stolen yellow 1963 Corvette convertible with black interior.

A shyster lawyer found some devious method of getting this degenerate reprobate out of prison 20 years before he was scheduled to be released. Got to love our criminal justice system.

It is a beautiful blue sky day with a few clouds to give the sky depth. A gentle breeze rustles the leaves but our man is unaware of any of this. He is concentrating on that nice looking girl who is wonderfully endowed with what God is so gracious to give to her.

She is driving in the car just ahead of him now. He noticed her assets as she passed him just a moment ago.

His interest is piqued, to say the least. It has been over a decade and a half since he has been with the girl who got him sent away.

He thinks to himself that the girl ahead of him in that car is twice again what that other girl had going on for herself. This here girl is prime real estate.

He is determined to have her. No matter what, when, where or how, he will take this girl. He must.

Oh my god, he can almost taste it. It will be wonderful. More than wonderful. It will be... Well, it is beyond words. Beyond at least his words.

They are approaching a railroad crossing. The man is hoping. Yes hoping that the gods are with him today.

They are getting closer and closer to the tracks.

And then it happens, the gods do shine upon him.

The crossing lights come on, the clanging begins and the gates begin to descend. He can hear the train whistle beginning to blare.

A broad smile comes upon his face. He can feel his manhood raging into a full-fledged attention. 'This is going to be wonderful,' he thinks.

Both cars begin slowing to a stop.

The loud rumbling engines are nearing the front end of the two cars.

The man is a fast thinker. He knows exactly what he is going to do. He realizes that the loud din with the clickity clackity of the wheels on the rails will distract the girl. This will allow him to slide over the center console, across to the passenger side and out the door.

He times his move to coincide with the passing train engines. He creeps up to the side of the girl's car and slowly opens the rear passenger door just as the loudest din is in front of the cars.

The ground is shaking and the ears are surrounded by the roar of the engines, the rattle of the rails and the blare of the horn makes his approach and entry invisible and silent.

As the engine noise moves onward and the railcars begin to pass in front of the girl's car, he springs up behind her with all the intentions of a man who has been in prison for longer than he cares to think.

The girl turns, looks at him and does a most peculiar thing.

She smiles a Cheshire cat smile.

A smile of one who knows something that no one else knows.

She is not in the least bit frightened. She is smiling with twinkling eyes.

Thomas realizes that there is something drastically wrong, 'Oh my god. What have I gotten myself into now? What is this wacked out broad grinning at? I am about to thoroughly enjoy myself with her regardless of what she wants or thinks about it. And she is smiling.

'My god she is almost laughing.

'What have I done? I have gotten myself a loony tunes. A wack-job. What floor did she escape from?'

The train, passes the gates go up and the clanging ends.

The girl drives away in her car, alone.

The yellow Corvette is still at the tracks with the passenger door open and the engine running. No one is seen anywhere. He is gone. Vanished.

2

A bit later that same day, three boys between the ages of 10 and 11 are walking along the railroad tracks kicking and throwing stones as they chat the chat of young boys.

The boys have summer haircuts for easy care. One is wearing shorts. The other two are wearing blue jeans. They are each wearing tee shirts of solid colors each different from the others. Tennis shoes finish the ensembles.

One of the boys carries a sling shot which he is practicing with using railroad track stones, aiming at various bushes and objects that he sees lying on the ground at various distances.

They walk this trail almost everyday both to and from school. It is also the shortcut to each of their houses.

They are very familiar with the tracks, the crossings, the requisite telephone poles and the surrounding brush and trees.

Thick brush and scrub trees make for a dense edging to the rails. Kind of like a walled-in set of tracks.

The day is still beautiful with the gentle breeze rustling the leaves.

As they approach the crossing they notice a fabulous yellow convertible with its passenger door open idling at the crossing.

They stop and admire the beautiful lines of the best sports car ever made.

They cross over the crossing and run up to it. They are more than a little curious because the engine is running.

"Wow". They all exclaim together.

'Hmm? What is going on though?'

'What is this great car doing here? Don't touch it. Remember about motorcycles and sports cars. Hands strictly off,' they seem to collectively say to themselves.

The boys do know better than to touch. But they can look and look they do.

It is a beautiful car. None has ever seen one before which makes this one all the better.

After as much time and attention that youth can put forth they continue on their way down the tracks.

The boy with the sling shot is aiming at a large grouping of bushes on his left. Suddenly, he stops, lowers the sling shot and stares at the side of the tracks where a break in the dense brush is seen. This is something new. What can have made the hole?

It is a jagged opening as if something or someone had torn their way through the brush. Something like a raging bull or a mad man went rampaging through bending and breaking the branches.

They each stare and none can figure it out.

They slowly approach the disrupted bushes and peer in. It is dark. They cannot make out a thing.

They decide to go through the opening. Just on the other side is a steep gully. They each slide down the bare back ridge to its bottom.

Their eyes adjust to the dimness and as their irises get big enough they can make out a body of a man lying on the ground.

There is blood on the ground near the man's head. A deep gash is seen where the blood had come from.

One of the boys, for some unknown reason, musters enough courage to approach the body.

He leans down, looks closely at the face and pronounces him dead.

"He looks dead."

Then-for whatever reason- he grabs an arm of the man, raises it and lets it drop. "Yep, D.E.A.D. Dead. See, I told you so."

At that moment the man's eyes fly open and a low guttural sound comes forth from his throat. He has eyes of a dead man.

The boys run.

CHAPTER ONE

(Present Day)

Matthew's plane is landing at the airport.

He is a pleasant looking man, often being told he is good looking and handsome. He does not think that those people have very good vision. They need better glasses. He has gray hair to accompany his sixty plus years of age. He has few wrinkles and has to watch out for too much sun. Sun is a no-no for him.

He is nearly six feet tall (or, at least, he used to be six foot but age tends to reduce a man's altitude, unfortunately). Maybe if we would stop jumping off roofs and trees in our youth. Never play football or "kill-the-man". *Maybe if we would eat better; better meaning foods that combat the production of free radicals in our bodies. These free radicals are unattached molecules that scientists say disrupt the body's normal functions and make them begin to malfunction thus causing aging.*

It has been a rather bumpy ride, resulting in having to wear the seatbelt the entire trip thus being unable to do the normal things that people do during five hour plane trips.

During the ride, and between the agonizing thoughts of not staying aloft, Matt pondered the cryptic message he had received from his childhood buddy, Luther.

It came in the form of a post card that was post-marked two days earlier. He remembered the day being cold, rainy and windy. Not a good day for being a postman.

The postcard is terse, due to the smallness of the card. It briefly reads, Matt, Urgent. Come quick. Digger is dead. Lute Matthew, being a Professor of Theology at the University, had definite ideas about death due to his extensive studies not only in the theological angle but also in the physiological.

He had contrived a theory combining the Christian Way of seeing the world and the dying process.

Matthew, being a Christian himself and a teaching professor to boot, knows of the peacefulness that accompanies a rightly believing follower of the One and only true God.

The concept of being able to put one's entire life into God's hands for all his needs and wants, without concern for the future, is calming for conducting one's life. Knowing that The Father will provide for you, all that He wishes for you is oh so very comforting.

This removes the burden of stress from one's life. This in turn reduces the amounts of free radicals in the body that contribute to the eventual destruction of humans.

Without God in one's life and without the hope for eventual entry into heaven, the human body becomes a hopeless empty shell. This empty hopelessness leads to eventual bodily destruction in various forms, including depression, sickliness, skin discoloration, sores, poor health, diseases, sluggishness, apathy and the list goes on and on.

Therefore, Digger's death held a lot of meaning to Matthew. They had been childhood friends all through school and had gone to the same undergraduate university; although they went off to different schools for graduate and doctoral universities.

During the years of post-graduate schooling they had stayed in touch; either by phone, letter and then emails, then texts.

They would see each other at each every-five-year class reunions, but as time wore on attendance to these waned.

It has been quite a while since the last correspondence and even longer since the last in-person conversation.

He considered the reality of never being able to even communicate with Digger let alone talk with him. It made him sad.

The two of them had been inseparable pals for over sixteen years in their youth. They had a bond which not many, in fact, very few ever had had.

Matthew is anxious to see Luther. Part of the anxiousness is because by then this horrible flight will be over.

CHAPTER TWO

Luther meets Matthew at the airport. It is a normal meeting between two old buddies. Hand-shakes, hugs and the obligatory 'how-was-the-trip' and 'it-is-so-good-to-see-you.' 'Thank you for coming.'

It is a surprisingly quiet ride to Lute's home. For some reason neither has anything to say. Each is wrapped up in their own thoughts. Matt is still recovering from the ride from Hell.

It is raining cats and dogs with the wind blowing the tops off the houses. Similar to the day he had received the post card. Kind of eerie.

Lute is having difficulty holding the car on track. But he does manage to navigate the car to its final destination, home.

Luther is the same age and height as Matthew. He is a nice looking man. He is a bit taller. He is somewhat bald. But to make up for the sparsely populated pate, the brown hair that he does grow grows at such a rate that he almost has to carry shears with him. The beard that he can produce makes the Smith Brothers proud. Girls think that his blue eyes are beautiful. And he enjoys wearing loose fitting comfortable cloths and practical foot wear.

Lute's home is in an out-of-the-way part of town. Not many houses are near.

It is the house he grew up in so Matt knows it well and feels normal and comfortable in it.

It looks pretty much the same as when they grew up except that the furniture has changed and the walls now have paint in places where the green and brown flowered paper had been on the walls.

"Matthew Thomas, you ol' hound dog." Lute calls from the kitchen. "It really is good to see you. You never did tell me about your flight other than saying, 'Hell cannot be worse.'"

Matt calls back, "Well, Luther St. Johns, I will tell you. It was the worst flight in the history of flights. The damn demons kept sucking the air out from underneath the plane, making it drop hundreds of feet. Then the thing would climb back up and repeat the drop again and again and again. It almost seemed that I should not have been on that flight."

"Want a drink?" Lute wants to know.

"You bet I do. Scotch will be terrific." Matt knew that Lute will have stocked up on Matt's favorite.

"I knew you would so I stocked up today."

Matt relaxing in the chair says, "Sure feels good to be back. How is the art doing?"

Lute replies, "Pretty darn good. I've got this great idea for a new type look for my pictures. It's going to-"

Matt cuts him off without thinking of what he just did. He blurts out, "I wish Digger hadn't died."

"Yeh, I know."

"How'd it happen?"

Lute responded, "It's kinda strange. The police can't quite figure it. There's something kinda odd. They say it almost doesn't look like an accident,"

Matt asks, "What do you mean it almost doesn't look like an accident?"

"Well, the skid marks were massive. He must have been going nearly a 100 when he rounded that corner. And there appeared to be beat marks all over the car. And one of the windows was smashed, but it could have happened from the crash. The police just don't know."

Lute comes in with the drinks, pausing at the doorway.

Lute asks, "Well?" He sips his beer.

"They do admit, well at least the ones who knew Digger, that they are confused about that speed. They knew Digger to be an overly cautious driver. They just don't get it."

"Well?" Matt asks again.

Lute gives Matt his drink and sits down in the cushy chair opposite Matt. He swigs his beer again as Matt sips his scotch on the rocks.

There is a bit of silence while each ponders their thoughts. Matt looks around the room, seeing Lute's paintings everywhere.

Lute is a very good accomplished artist. His mediums vary widely which makes him unique in the art world.

Most artists excel in one medium; Lute excels in multiple ones.

His best and favorite is oils. He loves the rich bold colors that only oils can afford.

His paintings come alive in the minds of the beholder. Some people almost pant when they gaze at his canvases. He is very very good at what he does.

He has sold dozens of his canvases to private collectors around the world as well as to the general public.

Every exhibit is waited for and looked upon as a major event of the season. The exhibit will stay for only one week but in that short time virtually all of his paintings will have been sold.

He also sells his pastels. His multi-mediums don't do as well but then again most of their kind doesn't sell very well, no matter who creates them.

He has ventured into marble and copper statues which can be seen in multiple municipalities across the Fruited Plain.

To say the least, Luther is very successful and along with that comes wealth. He does not show it though. He lives modestly and drives a beater that would make any cheap-skate proud.

Matt comments, "I see that you are having a beer. You told me that you had stopped."

Lute says back, "No. I'm no... Oh. Well. I didn't realize it." Lute takes a drink.

"You know," he continues, "I guess I have been drinking a bit since Digger... You know..." Lute takes another drink. "I was there when he did..." Lute takes another drink. "Died, that is."

Astonished, Matt says, "What! What are you saying? You were with Digger when he died? Oh my gosh! You did not say so. It must have been horrible."

Lute nods and says, "Well, he was all banged up, broken bones all over his body. He was a bit like Raggedy Andy. His insides were all messed up and all. He was on all kinds of meds and such- IVs, pills, traction and anything else they could think of to make him comfortable. He wasn't hurting or anything. Oh, I don't know. I mean I don't remember. I mean..."

He chugs the last of his bottle and heads to the kitchen calling out, "Need more?"

"No. I'm good for now," Matt calls back.

Luther returns with a fresh bottle, sits back down and resumes his narrative.

"I was in the room. At that time I wasn't paying much attention to him. I mean, I wasn't talking to him. In fact, I wasn't even looking at him. I was across the room looking out the window.'

"And then I heard it."

"Heard what?" Matt cried.

Lute just stared at Matt. Stared without saying a word. Just stared a knowing look.

Lute rubbed his face and continued, "It was just the two of us in the hospital room. He was lying there kinda groaning mumbling something. I could not understand his words and it was painful looking at him. So I continued to stare out the window."

"You see, digger hadn't said a word since the accident. That is part of why no one knows exactly what happened."

Lute paused.

Matt waited patiently sipping his scotch.

Lute continued, "A week earlier he told me..."

Matt waited.

"He said that he had been telling me about... hearing things."

"What kind of things?" Matt quietly asks.

"Remember when the three of us were walking by the tracks and we found that dead guy with his head smashed in?"

Matt nods his head and replies, "I'll never forget it. That was the single most terrifying moment of my life. Did you ever find out what it meant?"

"That's what is so terrifying." Lute takes a big swallow. "Digger..." He takes another swig.

"Digger, what?"

There is silence in the room. Matt begins to get a creepy feeling.

He breaks the silence and softly prods Lute by quietly asking, "What about Digger?"

Lute takes another drink and says, "Well... Remember that guy... When Digger lifted up his arm..." Lute takes a drink and continues, "And then Digger drops the arm... And then the guy breathed out?"

Silence.

Matte again breaks the silence. "Yes. I remember it. I remember it well. I remember it as if it were yesterday."

Silence.

Matt continues. "We figure that was when he really died. We were there when that guy died. Wow!"

More silence.

Lute says, "Well... Digger, being the coroner and the physician around here and all that... And being around dead and guys all the time. Well..."

Lute downs his bottle, goes to the kitchen and returns with a fresh one.

Matt says, "No. No. I'm fine. I don't need a freshener."

Lute stares.

Lute begins again, "Well..."

Matt cries out, "Well what?"

Lute says, "Well, he hears it?

"Hears what?"

Matt is exasperated with this staccato narrative. It is driving him nuts. He is used to succinct, terse responses in his classroom. He demands it. He reasons that the attention span of anyone is extremely short. Therefore, one needs to get to the point as quickly as possible before the listener begins to wander to greener-thought pastures.

Matthew takes a deep breath giving him time and allowing Lute to get himself together and calmed.

Lute has been getting fairly worked up. Matt watches Lute take another swig from the beer bottle. Lute had given up drinking years ago and had not a drop since. Until now.

"That sound. That thing we heard that sounded German or Latin or whatever."

"Digger told me that he had been hearing people say..."

Matt waited a moment. He is fairly certain he knows what Lute is about to say. Even still Matt asks, "Say what?"

Luther whispered out, "Anima!"

"What?" Matt exclaims. He stands up.

Lute quietly says, "I'm saying that Digger said that more than just our dead guy is saying Anima."

"Oh my God... What does it mean?"

"I don't know", Lute replies.

"I am not asking, what does it mean that people are saying it, I am asking what does the word mean?"

"I don't know that either. I've been thinking. Why in heaven's name are they saying it?" Lute says.

"Hmm"

Silence descends as they both ponder the meaning of the word and the why people are saying it.

Anima.

Matt begins pacing. He often paces when he thinks deep thoughts. He considers it part of his thinking process.

Matthew breaks the silence with, "This is creepy. Very creepy. I had said that when we heard the dead man really died, that it was the creepiest time of my life. This right here has just taken the ribbon."

Lute replies, "Here's something else. Digger said that not every person says it; most, but not all."

More silence.

Lute finishes his beer. Matt finishes his scotch. They both go into the kitchen to replenish.

Lute tosses the empty into the glass-only container and grabs a fresh one from the fridge.

Matt grabs some cubes and begins splashing scotch into the glass over the rocks. He stops half way through, looks at Lute and asks, "What does that mean? Most but not all? Why not all? Hmm." He tops off his glass.

Lute takes a swig and they both return to the living room.

While walking Lute asks, "Do you suppose this is some worldly thing?"

"What? Where'd that come from? What do you mean?"

Lute sits down in Matt's chair while Matt sits on the sofa.

Lute continues, "I mean, what is going on? Can it be happening just here or all over, or all over the world? Is it religious?"

Matt leans back, resting his head against a pillow. He takes a sip. "I have no idea. It doesn't sound like anything I've ever studied, heard or read about. I've been teaching theology classes for twenty five years. I've written books, text books and study guides. I've written commentaries on the great Christian theologians and Christian precepts."

He points over at the bookshelf where Lute keeps copies of all Matt's writings.

Matt continues, "Nothing, I mean nothing that I have learned or read even hints at anything like this."

Lute returns, "Maybe it's one of those Eastern religion kinda things. Maybe... it's a New Age kinda thing. You know, where this is something that is actually real. You know, where like all of us are connected and we're all a part of the universe and where somehow all our lives are a spark of energy that is tied to the universal something or other. You know what I mean?"

"No, but I appreciate the effort. I don't know much about modern-sophisticated-enlightened-thinking kind of stuff."

Lute says back, "I don't either."

Silence.

They each drink their drinks thinking about the bizarreness of this whole matter. Back when they were kids they ran across a dead guy who wasn't dead. While the boys watch, the man really does die. And as he dies, his last breath speaks what sounds like Anima.

Now it is being said that Anima is being heard from the dying lips of most people, not just their lone man way back then. Hmm.

Lute interrupts the thinking. "Matt? There is something else."

"What is it?"

Lute says, "Well... It has to do with what Digger said to me."

Matt looks over at Lute and gives him an exasperated look of 'Well, tell me?'

Lute goes on. "Well... It's that Digger has been coroner since... When? Six seven years after he became our local physician." Matt nods to encourage him. Lute continues, "Remember that church that got burned down by that group of wackos who kept saying that the church was not Christian but a church for the Evils? They kept saying Evils. Remember?"

"Yes, I remember a bit of that."

"Well, a few months ago, Digger talked about them. He sorta talked about them a lot. Nothing specific, he didn't know anything definite. He was just sorta... You know, he was sorta interested in them. You know the wackos and the Evils."

Matt chimed in with, "Yeh. He always liked conspiracies. Remember the Apollo Moon Landing conspiracy? And the Ke..."

"That right." Lute takes a swig and goes on.

"That church has been rebuilt."

Matt stares at him.

Lute goes on. "People are beginning to attend it again."

Matt continues to stare.

"This was two and a half or three years ago, or so," Lute says.

Matt is beginning to get a stirring of excitement. Digger was not the only one who liked this type story.

Lute then lays the bomb shell. "Digger says, 'that is when it started.'"

"When what started?"

"The Anima," Lute almost shouted. "DO YOU HEAR ME? Almost all the people started saying Anima as they died. This had not been happening until the church was rebuilt!"

They each take a healthy drink.

Matt stares at Lute and says, "Yes, and?"

Lute retorts, "Don't you see? This is what Digger was saying- the church has something to do with this Anima thing."

Matt asks, "How?"

Lute replies, "I don't know for sure. But I do know that Digger said that a whole heck of a lot of people started saying that word and he got to wondering, you know how he always did, if what those guys that burned the church down in the first place were right; that they did the right thing."

"Right what? That the church was for Evils or whatever? Get out of here."

Lute replies, "Why not? Digger started looking into the church and all that. You know- internet and library. He even went over there to look around. While he was there trying to look in a window, someone came up behind him. It startled the living bejeebers out of him; the guy had come from behind so quiet like.

Matt asked, "What did the fellow say?"

"Well, Digger asked the guy, 'When does church meet?'"

"The guy told him, 'they meet when they do and not at other times. But it's usually on a Tuesday.'"

Matt's eyes get big and they stare at Lute.

Lute says, "Digger tried to ask more stuff but the guy just turned and left."

Matt thought for a moment and then said, "That is pretty weird. What an odd thing to say, we meet when we do and not at other times. What do you make of it?"

Lute says, "I don't. I can't. I don't want to."

"What are you talking about? What do you mean?"

"What I mean is that Digger told me that after that he was being followed. Guys in the black church van would always be around wherever he went. You know, like to the store or his croaker lab or even his church. The van was always nearby. What do you think?"

Matt stood up again and began to pace, again. He said, "I think that... I do not know."

Luther says, "Well, let me tell you one more thing." Lute finishes his beer, goes back into the kitchen, opens the fridge, grabs a new cold one and returns to his seat in the living room.

Both take drinks. Matt goes to the kitchen for a refill. He returns and leans against the fireplace mantle.

Matt says after a few more moments of silence, "Let us find out."

"What?"

"Let us find out what Anima means."

Lute answers, "Why not find out about the church?"

Matt answers him with, "Two reasons. 1: I do not want to get dead. And 2: Knowing what Anima means will tell us a reason for the church being around."

"Oh, okay. How? Where?"

"Library."

CHAPTER THREE

Matthew Thomas and Luther St. Johns are heading to the library in Lute's car. It is the next morning and it is beautiful outside. A gentle breeze keeps everything fresh. Breakfast of hot black coffee, toast, jam and sunny-side-up eggs made for a feast for the kings.

They had just left Lute's neighborhood heading toward the library which is down town just off Main St on Pine.

They drive past the park. It is a great little park for a town this size. It has a few ballparks for all the different ages. It also has a soccer field, a horse shoe toss area and tennis courts. There are wooded areas and grassy areas for picnicking or doing whatever one wants to do on the grass. Circling and weaving in and around the venues is a running and biking trail. All together it is two and a half miles long.

Lute says as he points toward the running trail, "Hey, that's Janey Hoskins. Remember her? She was that cute little girl who delivered the newspaper on her roller skates."

Matt replies, "Ah, so that is who that is. How did she get so big? I remember her as being a really nice looking little girl."

Lute says, "Yeh. She seemed like one of those truly good people."

Matt returns, "Wow! Look at her now." What Matt sees is a very overweight girl with long, stringy, dark brown hair. She basically looks unkempt; but her eyes are a beautiful blue.

Lute says, "Let's go talk to her,"

"Alright."

The car pulls up to Janey as Luther rolls down his window. Luther leans out and says, "Janey, guess who I have here with me in the front seat?"

Janey bends down to peer into the car and remarks, "He looks kinda familiar."

"Hi Janey. I am Matthew. Matthew Thomas"

Janey looks a bit unsure. It has been a long time between sightings.

Matthew eases her unsureness with, "Matthew Thomas. Remember? I am the one who-"

"Oh yes!" Janey said excitedly. "You're the one I hit on the head with the folded up newspaper. I threw it just as you opened the door. I wasn't looking and you didn't see me. I was really sor-"

Matthew once again eases Janey's angst with, "That was one of the funniest things. I tell that story, still, in some of my classes at the University. I tell it during the lectures on The Second Coming. You know, 'be prepared.' I was not."

Janey smiles, nods and says, "Wow! That is pretty cool. At college. I remember that you went into that goofy Inspector Clouseau karate stance thing. I still chuckle when I think of it."

Luther interrupts the revelry by asking Janey, "How far are you running today?" Luther thinks, to himself, that she should probably go ten miles to help get rid of that extra seventy pounds she has put on.

"I'm only doing five miles today. I'm doing twelve tomorrow, though. I'm getting ready for the WHEELCHAIRS FOR ALL marathon in three weeks."

Luther asks, "How many sponsors do you have?"

Just then, behind Janey, in the distance, a figure of a man is seen walking out from among the trees. From this distance the man is not recognizable.

He appears to be just standing there gazing about. However, every now and then he will glance over at the girl and the car, or at least in their direction.

Janey says, "Only thirty nine sponsors so far. That's only good for thirty nine wheelchairs. I need a lot more. It's so sad that all those third world people have to live on the ground with no way to get around but to crawl. I want to do more. I want to give mobility to as many of those poor people as I can. I hurt so much when I think of them."

Luther says, "Janey, you've done quite a lot already for the cause. What is thirty nine chairs times $50 per chair?"

Matthew says after a moments pause, "About $1700 dollars. That does sound pretty darn good."

Luther continues, "That's more than anyone else has gotten so far, isn't it?"

In a bit of self-deprecation, Janey replies, "Oh, I don't know. I guess so. I can still do more, though."

"Janey," Matthew says, "put me down for five chairs. $200."

"Gee, thanks Mr. Thomas."

"Please Janey. I am proud of you," says Matthew.

Luther says to Janey, "Well, keep it up. Run well. It is nice seeing you. Catch you later. Bye."

Janey calls back as the car moves slowly in the direction of the man, "Bye."

Both Luther and Matthew glance at the man, for no particular reason, like people do when they pass someone, as they drive by. He is nondescript; not too short, not too tall. Not too fat, not too thin. His facial features are ordinary; nothing to remember. His clothes are ordinary, everyday, outside clothes. He wears a T shirt, jeans and tennis shoes.

Luther looks back at the man through the rear view mirror. Matthew reflects back at the man though the side mirror.

Janey begins running. She apparently does not notice the man near the path as she starts her run. She is concentrating on getting her ear buds put in.

As she nears the figure, he comes onto the path. Janey notices the figure, now, coming towards her. She gives him a slight polite wave.

As she gets nearer and nearer she notices that the sounds of the birds and of the children playing and the traffic is getting quiet. And as she gets right up to him she notices that the man's chest rises as if inhaling a deep breath. Then there is no sound at all.

Immediately, she hears a slurping sound; the sound of a straw sucking up the remains of a liquid in the bottom of a can. It ends with an echoing hollow sound.

She passes him. Janey keeps running. The figure keeps walking.

Luther and Matthew observe all of this and think nothing out of the norm. They cannot see Janey's face. They are too far away.

CHAPTER FOUR

A small group of Moslems are congregated in chairs at a round table on the sidewalk in front of THE OLDE WORLD CAFE. They are chattering away, drinking their tea and watching the world go by.

These are all male. Not a female to be seen among them. Some are wearing definite Arab garb. Others are wearing American type clothing.

Lute and Matt pass them as they head toward the library. Matt stares at them as they wait at the red light.

Lute takes off on green. Matt slowly shakes his head. He sighs. He says, "It is such a shame about Muslims. Or, for that matter, any other of the religions such as Hindu, Buddhism, Confucianism, Shinto and Baha'i. Or Metaphysics, Transcendental Meditation, Atheism and Navajo."

Lute pulls into a parking space at the side of the road. He can tell that Matt is about to go into a doozy.

"There are nineteen major religions in the world." Matt continues. "These are broken down into two hundred seventy large religious groups. In fact, since the resurrection, it is estimated that there have been about forty thousand denominations of the world's religions."

"It is a bit mind boggling that each religion, each denomination, each sect 'knows' that their way is the way. Whether you become a cow next time or you just die and are gone into nothingness, each knows that their way of religion is the answer to why we are alive."

"Being a Christian has a caveat that the other religions do not necessarily have. Christianity has it that belief in Jesus as the Son of God Who is the creator of the universe is a prerequisite for being a true Christian."

"Christianity has it that the reason for our lives is that 1) it is pleasing to God, 2) for us to praise God and 3) enjoy doing so. Other religions require things to be done or accomplished in order to attain a level of self- enlightenment to be able to be self-actuated. Or, in other words, to have made it."

"Jesus said that belief in Him is paramount. Basically, it is only through Him that one will or can enter heaven. And heaven is the prize for being a Christian. It is not the goal. It is the result of being a true Christian."

"Approximately one thousand Christian denominations compete for the laity in the United States. Not all of these Christian denominations are actually Christian. Some do not hold that Jesus is the true Son of God; that He is a very good prophet, only. Others will allow different methods for entering heaven; such as doing good deeds and having someone forgive your sins for you."

"That is neither here nor there. I have gotten a bit far afield," Matt comments. "Getting back to the matter at hand which is one's belief in the One True God."

Matt goes right back at it with, "The Bible gives the Jews the Ten Commandments.

The first commandment reads:
You shall have no other gods before me.
The second commandment reads:
You shall not make for yourself an idol, or any likeness of what is in heaven above or on the earth beneath or in the water under the earth. You shall not worship them or serve them; for I, the LORD your God, am a jealous God, visiting the iniquity of the fathers on the children, on the

third and the fourth generations of those who hate Me, but
showing lovingkindness to thousands, to those who love Me
and keep My commandments.

"Putting these two together tells us that He, God, is the One and only. Since God came to earth in the form of Jesus, then belief in Jesus is the only way to go. In other words, those who do not believe in the Christian God believe in a man-made religion that holds no water at all. It is a waste of their time."

"When push comes to shove, they will lose out."

"That is what I was thinking about as I saw those Muslims. They are going to be on the outside of heaven's gates at the end times. It is such a waste of humanity. Their souls will be lost for all eternity as will the others."

Lute says, "I know one of them in that group. His name is Ishmael Mohammad. He is a nice, kind man. He's one of those guys who will help the little old lady cross the street."

Matt says, "I feel doubly sorry for him. He does not have Jesus in his life. Therefore, no matter how good a person he or anyone else is in this world, they are on the wrong side of the fence." Curiously, as they sit there, a well-dressed older woman passes the group of Muslims. She slows just a bit and looks directly at them.

Her shoulders rise as if she is inhaling. A few look up at her as she passes. Matt notices a strange change come upon their faces. He is too far away to see what the actual change is.

Lute pulls away from the curb and they continue their journey to the library.

CHAPTER FIVE

Matthew and Luther arrive at the library.

Two young girls are walking together. They are passing in front of the library. They are dressed as they will dress- short shorts, tight tank tops and sandals. It is a bit provocative.

They walk past a nicely dressed man in business attire without even noticing him. They do not notice the rise in the man's shoulders as if he is inhaling. They do, though, experience the same hearing anomalies that Janey went through.

Their hearing begins to fade. When there is complete silence, they immediately hear a slurping sound; the sound of a straw sucking up the remains of a liquid in the bottom of a can. It ends with an echoing hollow sound.

An elderly gentleman on a handicap electric scooter is leaving the library. He is wearing gray baggy trousers typical of older men, he has a red, blue and yellow plaid long sleeve shirt and brown tie shoes with white socks. He is smiling with a friendly gentlemanly smile.

A young, pretty girl in her twenties that is nicely dressed stops and holds the door for him. She is pretty with that youthful kind of prettiness. Her hair is a straight, long blond. She has stylish white shorts and a purple golf shirt. Her smile shows perfect teeth. Thank goodness for orthodontics.

As the wheelchair bound man passes through the door, his hearing begins to fade. He notices that the pretty girl seems to be inhaling; her shoulders are rising.

When there is complete silence, he immediately hears a slurping sound; the sound of a straw sucking up the remains of a liquid in the bottom of a can. It ends with an echoing hollow sound.

Luther and Matthew pass the old man and the girl as she holds the door for them. Luther nods and smiles a thank you to the young girl. She returns a sweet pleasant smile to them.

Matthew nods to the old man. *Wait a minute*, he says to himself. *What was with that guy's eyes? They looked blank. Dead. Non-seeing. Must be nothing. Just the eyes of an elderly man.*

But wait a minute; those two girls had the same dead eye look on their faces. What is up with that?

Matt keeps this thought to himself. He wants to work on it before saying anything to Lute.

They continue on into the library.

CHAPTER SIX

Their quest, their goal is to discover what the word Anima is or what it means. Matthew is sure that this is the place to begin.

The dead people themselves cannot be much help. The one thing in common is Anima. So it is Anima or bust.

Matthew leads the duo to the reference section of the library. Here he hopes that they will find what they are looking for; in this case he does not know what it will be. This can be a bit exciting if one looks at this as an adventure.

Luther goes for the dictionary first and searches for Anima.

"How do you spell the dang word anyway? Aneema doesn't work. How about annema. No. Let me try anemma. No, that can't work. Can't have a long e with a double m. Let me try animma. No. Well that leaves anima. Tada! Yay!"

He announces to Matt that he has found it and reads the first definition out loud. This piques Matt's interest.

Matt suggests that he write it down. And they will take everything back to Lute's place and cull through it in the comfortable living room with the aid of their buddies Scotch and Beer.

This is what Luther writes:

Anima [**an**-uh-muh] - noun

1. Soul; life.
2. (in psychology of C.G. Jung)

    1. The inner personality that is turned toward the unconscious of the individual (contrasted with persona).
    2. The feminine principle, especially as present in men (contrasted with animus).

Animus [**an**-uh-muhs] -noun

1. Strong dislike or enmity; hostile attitude; animosity.
2. Purpose; intention, animating spirit.
3. (In the psychology of C. G. Jung) the masculine principle, especially as present in women (contrasted with anima).

While Lute is making his discoveries, Matt begins his quest. Lute's research and reading of the first definition gives him direction.

He searches and finds A Handbook of Theological Terms. He does not find Anima. He does find Animism.

He writes down what he found:

Animism. *The belief that all natural phenomena are possessed of souls of spirits that animate them and explain their special characteristics.*

In the Pocket Dictionary of THEOLOGICAL TERMS he also finds Animism with a much larger description. He of course knows he needs to copy this also:

Animism. A system of belief that asserts that spirit beings are the cause of all movement, growth or change (animation) in the world, although many animists acknowledge one most powerful god, they are highly sensitive to the presence of the spiritual world. Animists, therefore, would explain various movements, such as the growth of a tree, the rustling of its leaves and the shedding of its leaves, as visible effects of invisible spirits.

Matthew briefly ponders what they have come up with so far. There seems to be a pattern developing that may give them a direction to take.

He searches through a Bible Dictionary, finding nothing. So to his way of thinking, Anima is not a Christian or Jewish term. But that does not mean it has nothing to do with theological things, though. He will keep an open mind.

He suggests to Lute that he look up the word soul. This is what he finds:

Soul [sohl] -noun

1. the principle of life, feeling, thought and action in humans, regarded as a distinct entity separate from the body, and commonly held to be separable in existence from the body; the spiritual part of humans as distinct from the physical part.
2. the spiritual part of humans regarded in its moral aspect, or as believed to survive death and be subject to happiness or misery in a life to come: arguing the immortality of the soul.

Matt calls for the end of the research for the time being. He tells Lute that they have enough data to begin an in depth study into the recent goings on of the people gasping out Anima as they breathe their last. Pretty creepy.

CHAPTER SEVEN

They head out the front doors of the library. It is late afternoon; the sun is in the western sky sending long shadows to the east. A pleasant temperature helped by a gentle breeze from the northwest makes the late afternoon a most pleasant.

Matt remembers back to his younger days and the late spring and early autumn days. They seemed to be always this way. What a wonderful place to grow up. It is a shame that his University is not in Salem. That would be nice.

When they get about half way down the steps they hear a familiar voice calling out to any person whom he knows or whom he just meets. This is the deacon of the main protestant church in town.

Deacon, named Johnathon Christian III (JC to everyone; friend or foe) is a very important person in the church and in the community. Not only is he the head of the Board of Deacons for the church, he is also an Alderman for the town.

Matthew and Luther look and see JC glad-handing and slapping people on their backs. JC is all smiles and praises to God; praise for such a beautiful day and praise God for such a beautiful baby. And "Hey Joe, praise God that your wife has gotten well from that horrible illness."

JC is dressed in an immaculate gray suit with a long-sleeved button down white shirt. Around his neck is his tie sporting the Yale colors, which he likes to wear most likely because he likes showing off the fact that he went there for his undergraduate degree. His ultra-shiny brogues are black. He of course has black socks on. The white carnation in his left lapel completes the package known as JC.

Lute leans over to Matt and in a conspiratorial tone says, "Boy, you should hear him on the golf course. You hear lots of, 'Praise God for that putt. Praise God for that tree. Praise God for that short patch of rough near the green.'"

"He makes it sound as if he is God's Chosen One. He sounds so righteous."

"I saw him at church last Sunday. He was a greeter at the door. He was praising everyone for everything for what God has done for them."

"He was at a charity fund raiser a few weeks back, praising God for the generous donations that people made. He made a big loud attention drawing announcement about his donation. However, it is rumored it wasn't as generous as the others."

"But this is neither here nor there. He certainly seems like a very spiritual man. However, he does make a few people feel uncomfortable and inadequate because they can't come close to the holiness that JC puts forth. But I am certain that he means well."

What Luther does not know about JC is that when Johnathon Christian is not with people he is a much different person.

For instance, upon dropping an egg onto the kitchen floor instead of into the frying pan he swears up a blue streak. He may even throw things in his hot temper anger.

He will kick the dog for being in the way, and his aquarium has been restocked three times due to lack of care.

His wife died in a fatal car accident so he doesn't have to put up with "that" anymore. His son never calls nor does he call him. Neither visits each other.

He rarely prays. When he does pray, it is for status and he thanks God for his pious attitude.

Actually, he rarely thinks about God at all; even when he is publicly praising God.

He does not, at all, live up to his moniker, JC.

Matthew and Luther continue to stand on the steps watching the show from across the street.

JC finally wishes God's blessing onto the last of the group of people and marches on down the sidewalk.

Down near the corner quite a distance away is a figure of a man. The distance is far enough that virtually no features are discernible but he is well dressed.

JC is walking in that direction.

As JC nears the man, for some reason, he slows down a bit. It may have been an unconscious slowing or may have been deliberate.

As JC comes close, he notices that his ears begin to hear less and less. As he comes abreast of the man, there is complete silence. The man's chest enlarges as if inhaling. Immediately, he hears a slurping sound; the sound of a straw sucking up the last of a liquid in the bottom of a can. It ends with an echoing hollow sound.

Matthew and Luther observe the walking of JC and his passing the man but noticed nothing to pique their curiosity. If they had been able to see JC's face, they would have seen the eyes go blank, as if dead.

CHAPTER EIGHT

On the way back to Lute's house they stop in at the convenience store just on the edge of town.

They need to pick up a few things such as coffee for the morning wake up, bacon and eggs for the fast breaking, and orange juice because it tastes so good.

Luther opens the door to enter, but first he holds it open for an old man in a wheelchair. The chair wheels out of the store passing Luther and comes face to face with Matthew.

Matthew immediately recognizes him as the dead-eyed man at the library. And, yes, that man definitely has the eyes of a dead man.

Creepy.

The two stare at each other for a short moment, then Matthew gives a slight nod to the man. The man returns it with a slight friendly smile.

The man passes and Lute leads the way into the store because he knows where everything is. He grabs a basket and heads for the cold case.

The store has quite a few people milling up and down the aisles. Matt recognizes three of them. They were part of that group of Moslems in the front of THE OLDE WORLD CAFE restaurant.

Staring at them, his jaw almost falls open. He is staring at three pairs of dead-looking eyes on the three Moslems. Dead eyes like the wheel chair man's. Matt is dumb struck. *What is going on?*

He gathers himself and catches up to Lute.

In the third aisle they meet the owner.

The owner is a severely attractive woman in her early forties. However, she looks nearer fifty. Her name is Zoya.

Zoya immediately puts on a big happy smile as she does for all the customers.

She is dressed in comfortable casual clothing consisting of tennis shoes with light yellow peds, soft looking comfortable light green slacks, a yellow Toledo Swiss Dot sleeveless blouse. She thinks of herself as *styling*.

She greets and thanks them for stopping in. Lute introduces Matt to her with, "Matt is here for a few days. He is also a childhood friend of Digger's. The three of us were inseparable growing up. We did everything together."

After shaking hands she asks, "And what is it that you do to keep yourself out of trouble?"

"And who says I do stay out of trouble?"

All three chuckle.

Matt says, "You keep a very nicely organized shop. Everything looks so nice and fresh. And clean. Congratulations."

"Well, thanks," she replies. "I owe it all to my employees. They are great."

Matt says, "That is good of you to say. It was nice meeting you. Bye."

Lute says, "Bye."

"Bye", she says, heading toward the back of the store.

Lute and Matt picked up what they needed including beer. Because Zoya is such a nice person Matt picks out a Single Malt Scotch from here instead of at the less expensive Liquor Store.

They leave.

There are no longer any customers in the store, but if there were they would have heard Zoya rail at and belittle her employees. Zoya is not a nice person.

She is reminding them of the fact that they certainly need her a hell of a lot more than she needs them. She can always get new workers a hell of a lot easier than they can get a new job. Especially the way they work.

She says to them in a loud condescending voice, "You two have got to be the laziest worthless workers that God has ever put onto this earth. I am certain that he is ashamed of you."

The two workers look at each other.

She goes on, "Now, about Sundays. You two are now required to work on Sunday. The new hours for each of you are now seven and a half hours a day, five days a week. And no over time. Well, you know how it is. With the economy being so bad and as you know, I have to make a little bit of profit."

The employees look at each other both thinking the same thing, *Zoya has cut our hours. Ouch! She is going to save on unemployment taxes and benefits. The witch.*

Zoya continues, "I was just talking to a customer who noticed that the floors are messy and the shelves are unkempt. Listen here, if you two want to keep your jobs, you had better straighten up right now."

She ends with, "Now get out there and do a better job."

The two slowly go back out to their duties and Zoya heads to the cash register. It is time to count the drawer.

As she approaches the counter, a man comes through the door ringing the door chime as he enters.

He is a rather nicely dressed man in jeans, a solid dark green t-shirt, white socks and tennis shoes. He has shortish brown hair combed with a part on the left side. The man slowly heads toward the cash register and toward Zoya.

Zoya gets to the register just before the man does. She notices that her hearing is fading. As she looks up at the approaching man, Zoya notices that the man is taking in a deep breath.

When the man stands directly in front of her, there is no sound at all. The man's chest enlarges as if inhaling. Immediately she hears a slurping sound; the sound of a straw slurping the last of the liquid from the bottom of a can. It ends with an echoing hollow sound.

Just at that moment one of the employees peeks around the corner of the aisle.

The worker can see the back of a man but cannot see Zoya at all. The view is blocked. The worker goes back to work.

If the worker had waited a moment longer, he would have seen the man turn and leave, revealing Zoya staring at nothing with her now blank, dead, empty eyes.

CHAPTER NINE

Lute is now driving Matt through the familiar neighborhoods of their youth taking a nostalgic tour. They drive past the Stefansson's house, then the Persinger house and Talbot house, as well as the Taggart, Pease, Offensen, Bowman and Barton houses.

There are such great memories from one of the greatest experiences of growing up ever experienced in the history of mankind.

Matt and Lute reminisce about how the whole neighborhood would play the kick the can game. They played kickball and wiffleball. They played hide and seek.

They rode their bikes everywhere- to the store, to each other's house. They would organize bank robberies where they would go down to the cemetery and divide the loot which was often the horse chestnuts that they picked from the tree behind Old Man Thompson's house.

Each of these things was done by almost every child growing up in neighborhoods, but Matt and Lute knew that theirs was the best of any of them.

They continue on. Lute points out the old Foster house which was sold to a single Mom a few years ago. Lute remarks, "She seems like a nice enough lady. She has a daughter who seems rather nice, also. I've never spoken to her, though, so I don't really know."

Inside the home is another story. The adolescent daughter is one of the nastiest, most hurtful children to live on this earth.

The Mom works a day job down at the cannery. It is tedious smelly work, but she needs the job to survive. She also takes in laundry in the evenings to help make the ends meet.

Every morning Mom will leave a note on the refridge giving instructions of little duties for her daughter to do when she gets home from school. Things such as: Please do the dishes. Please separate the clothes in the laundry room. Please set the table for supper.

These are the type of tasks that Mom asks the daughter to perform to help out around the house and to ease the burden.

Today is no different from any other day. Mom has left a note.

She reads the job list and says out loud, "It will be a cold day in hell before I do any of these silly things." She rips up the note.

She is dressed like a girl who has little regard for herself. Shrinks might say that she suffers low self-esteem. She is wearing very baggy, saggy, and very-worn sweat pants, a grungy orange tank top, no socks or shoes.

Her long brown hair is uncombed from her sleeping on it all night. Her face is a bit shiny as if she didn't bother to wash it this morning.

She grabs some food from the refridge, heads into the den, puts her feet up on the coffee table, grabs the phone, dials her girlfriend and begins eating and dropping crumbs with every bite.

She immediately begins tell her girlfriend that her Mom has left another silly little task note and starts to laugh.

The doorbell rings. This irritates the girl to no end. She is busy.

The bell rings again.

She sighs the sigh of "whatever" and trudges to the front door.

As she approaches the screened front door, she sees a man on the porch. He looks like a decent man; nicely dressed in jeans, solid dark green t-shirt and white socks and tennis shoes. He has shortish brown hair combed with a part on the left side.

She calls out, "Yeh. What d'ya want?"

She hears a mumble.

She calls out this time sarcastical and slowly, "Whaaaat doooo youuuu waaaant?"

She hears through the door, "You, my dear. I want you." Followed by a slight chuckle.

She doesn't know it nor does it mean anything to her, but this man on her front porch is the same nicely dressed man who was just at the convenience store meeting Zoya.

The man's chest enlarges as if inhaling.

Her hearing disappears and she hears a slurping sound; a sound of a straw sucking the liquid from the bottom of a near empty can. It ends with an echoing hollow sound.

CHAPTER TEN

Lute and Matt make it back to the house where Lute puts the groceries away. He pours a single malt scotch into a rocks glass with ice, grabs a beer and heads in to the dining room. Matt is at the table with their papers from the library.

Lute hands Matt his scotch and takes a seat beside him. He sips his beer and Matt sips his scotch.

They silently read over the papers in front of them. They read once again:

Anima [**an**-uh-muh] - noun

3. soul; life.
4. (in psychology of C.G. Jung)

   2. The inner personality that is turned toward the unconscious of the individual (contrasted with persona).
   3. The feminine principle, especially as present in men (contrasted with animus).

Animus [**an**-uh-muhs] -noun

4. Strong dislike or enmity; hostile attitude; animosity.
5. Purpose; intention, animating spirit.
6. (in the psychology of C. G. Jung) the masculine principle, especially as present in women (contrasted with anima).

Animism. *The belief that all natural phenomena are possessed of souls of spirits that animate them and explain their special characteristics.*

Animism. *A system of belief that asserts that spirit beings are the cause of all movement, growth or change (animation) in the world, although many animists acknowledge one most powerful god, they are highly sensitive to the presence of the spiritual world. Animists, therefore, would explain various movements, such as the growth of a tree, the rustling of its leaves and the shedding of its leaves, as visible effects of invisible spirits.*

Soul [sohl] -noun

3. the principle of life, feeling, thought and action in humans, regarded as a distinct entity separate from the body, and commonly held to be separable in existence from the body; the spiritual part of humans as distinct from the physical part.
4. the spiritual part of humans regarded in its moral aspect, or as believed to survive death and be subject to happiness or misery in a life to come: arguing the immortality of the soul.

"Anima is not a Christian or Jewish term," Matt reminds the two of them. "This is interesting because it talks of the soul but not religiously."

Matt goes on, "The definitions mention Jung. Carl Jung was a famous Swiss psychiatrist and psychologist. He founded analytical psychology. He was also influential in philosophy, anthropology, archaeology, literature and religious studies."

"He developed," Matt continues, "the integration of opposites: extraversion and introversion, conscious and unconscious and the masculine principle in women and the feminine principle in men."

"Well, thinking about Carl Jung along with his contributions to mankind, I believe we can discount his principles from our equation. Do you agree?" Matt asked.

"Yes. I agree. It does not seem to have any bearing on what we have before us which is: Dying people gasping out Anima on their last breath," Lute offers.

"Yes," agrees Matt. "That leaves us with: soul, life and animism. Hmm."

"Animism has some good possibilities," Matt says after some thought. "At first glance it has principles related to theology. The concepts that spirit beings or spirits, if you like, are the driving force behind everything; consciousness, movement, thinking and etc. Everything is governed by spirits.

"Christians think of soul as spirit. Remember; 'Let us make man in our image...' God being a spirit though having taken a body for a time in allowing Jesus to live upon the earth as man, God is still a spirit. It is in this spirit image that we, man, is in the image of God. In Jesus, God took the image of us, man."

Lute interrupts, "That is pretty cool. Did you just come up with that?"

Matt says, "No. This has been going around for a very long time; centuries."

"It goes on to say that man's existence is for communication with God through our spirit; from one spirit to another spirit," Matt finishes.

He does go on with, "Man has a spirit as do animals but it is we who realize it and are able to communicate with God."

"God created conscious life. He created our bodies which die and He created our spirit which is us, who we are," concluded Matt.

"So", Lute says, "We are two parts; body and spirit? Right?"

But before Matt can reply, which was not necessary anyway, Lute continues. "The spirit or soul? Is what you are saying?"

Matt says, "Yes. Yes indeed."

There is a pause, allowing each to take a drink of their preferred beverages. Lute is considering what has been said. Matt is thinking about what the next logical sequence should be in this mini lecture.

Matt takes a healthy sip and continues, "I think our discussion has eliminated animism out of the equation."

"Animism talks about a spirit or spirit beings running everything or causing everything to happen. This spirit is not referring to the Christian soul but actual beings separate from humans. Not actually a part of man."

Matt goes on with, "What our spirit is referring to is our soul. That part of us we call us, ourselves, our personality; who we truly are. It is this soul that enables us to know to communicate with God."

"The soul is what makes each of us unique from another. Our soul includes our likes and dislikes, our aptitudes and abilities. It includes our wants and desires, our strengths and weaknesses, our emotions and anything else that makes us who we are. All of these are within our soul. It is our personality."

Lute is agog. He has never heard things quite like this before. He has never thought of the souls as having so much depth. He basically had thought of the soul as that spark of life that God breaths into each of us and will live on into heaven.

Matt says, "So the soul is so very important to any man-for it is who he is and how he is. And to finish it, the 'in God's image...' Our soul is very important to each of us. The soul is the image of God."

Lute chimes in with, "So animism is out and Anima is in. Animus is also out because it does not at all fit with what we have going here."

He takes a drink. Finishes the bottle returns to the kitchen for another one.

On his way back in he says, "That leaves us with Anima. Anima means soul. But, what about it?"

They ponder this conundrum. Yes. What about it?

Matt rises and goes to the kitchen for a refill. He returns and takes a comfortable chair in the corner facing the kitchen.

Matt begins slowly, "We are now not what God intended. When Adam tasted of the tree of Good and Evil, Adam died. He had a spiritual death. We can see this in the fact that he and Eve hid from God when He came to them in the Garden. Prior to the sin, Adam and Eve and God walked together and talked together."

"And we have been hiding from Him ever since. We have slowly lost our sense of identity and we lash out at others and our minds decay. The Apostle Paul talks about it in Romans 1:21-23, 'For even though they knew God, they did not honor Him as God or give thanks, but they became futile in their speculations, and their foolish heart was darkened. Professing to be wise, they became fools, and exchanged the glory of the incorruptible God for an image in the form of corruptible man and of birds and four-footed animals and crawling creatures. Therefore God gave them over in the lusts of their hearts to impurity, so that their bodies would be dishonored among them. For they exchanged the truth of God for a lie, and worshiped and served the creature rather than the Creator, who is blessed forever.'" "From this we can see that man has fallen from grace quite a distance. We have fallen so far that many people do not know or even recognize God for Who and What He is: the creator of all. And this creator is our Father. As with any father, He wants what is best for each of us in our own ways. He also wants us to return to Him in heaven when we die." At this, Lute says, "So, it is our soul that is really us. It is our soul which communicates to God. It is our soul that God will take back to Himself when we die. Right? Right. Your education has done you good, my boy." "Thank you." "Hey, Lute, there is something that I need to tell you. I have been thinking about for a little bit. Do you remember the man in the wheelchair whom you held the door for down at the convenience store? We saw him once before." "Where?" "The library, remember?" "Vaguely. So?" "Well, I remember him because when we saw him at the convenience store I looked at his eyes. They had that dead look to them. I remember wondering about them when I saw him at the library. Dead eyes." And I saw three of the Moslems from THE OLDE WORLD CAFE. They also had dead looking eyes." Matt continues, "Remember that non-dead guy back when we were kids? Before he took his actual last breath and said 'Anima', he had those same dead eyes. Remember?" "Yes, I do remember. How can any of us forget? I still wake up seeing it in my mind's eye and when I go to bed. Maybe that is why I was drinking so much. I was trying to black out the memory of it so that I could go to sleep." They both sat in silence enwrapped in their own thoughts. Lute breaks the silence with, "I now remember the wheeled chair guy. You are right. The dead eyes are the same." "OH MY GOSH! What does this mean?" "Now, Lute, I can't know for sure but it does seem to fit with what we have discovered about Anima. When we die, our soul immediately leaves our body. And the eyes turn dead." Lute interrupts him saying," But these people aren't dead. They are alive. Alive, as much as you and I? So how can they have dead eyes and be alive at the same time?" Matt responds with," That I have not figures out yet. It does not seem possible, if indeed these people do have dead eyes, how can they be alive with them?" "Maybe they just look like the dead eyes from when we were kids. Maybe they are diseased eyes or really tired eyes", Lute says. "Yes, maybe. Let us think about this more. Maybe something new will come up." Lute says," Hey, let's keep a closer eye on people. Maybe something will come to us." "Good idea."

CHAPTER ELEVEN

During the time that Luther and Matthew are chewing and digesting all that they know about Anima and people, a guy is standing outside of a bar smoking an unfiltered Lucky Strike. It used to be filtered but he tore the thing off.

He is a wisp of man so frail that even a gentle wind would knock him over. He is poorly dressed but acceptable for the bar he is standing outside of.

He has left his beer on the bar and has come outside for his smoke. When he finishes with his coffin nail, he intends to return to his stool and finish his waiting glass of beer and order another one. His smoke tastes and feels good to him. He has been smoking since he was a young boy on the farm. Cigarettes weren't easy to come by out there in the boonies away from any other farm.

He would take some from his step-father and step-mother who both smoked. His parents left him for adoption when he was three so, he doesn't remember them at all. Too bad for them. Too bad for him he thinks. But he doesn't really care one way or another. This is what he was dealt. These are the cards he is going to play. And the hell with them all. Everyone.

He does remember all of the foster homes he passed through. Any and all of the horror stories about those homes are true. You do not want to be a part of that system. Stay away.

Bumming cigarettes became a way of life. He never had money of his own so OPs (Other Peoples) were his only option. Yes, he had seen the posters and the ads for anti-smoking. He'd read about addiction and the cancer dangers. He was always saying "Ah! What the hell. What's it matter anyway? We're all going to die some time. I might as well enjoy myself in the meantime." He hacks and wheezes and spits out a really big one. He thinks that that loogie is one for the records. He finishes his smoke, flicks it into the street, blows out the last of the smoke and returns to his awaiting throne at the bar.

He sits there nursing his beer. He is beginning to crave another cigarette. As with many smokers, when they drink they tend to smoke more often. In his case, he now smokes two packs in place of the normal one pack. He is drinking and drinking requires of him to smoke twice as much as normal. Now that he thinks about it, he usually smokes two packs a day now that he is hitting his favorite bar nearly every day around 2 p.m. He leaves when he can barely walk. The time varies. It doesn't really matter. He has nothing else to do. As he sits there, new patrons come in; old patrons go out. There is a constant ebb and flow. He will often squint his eyes so that he can only see shadows. He stares into the mirror on the other side of the bar and tries to guess who is coming and going. One he can always get right is the guy in the wheel chair. He is an easy one. He is short and he glides instead of lopes. It's fun. A brand new man enters. Most of the patrons look to see who it is as they all do whenever anyone enters the bar, or any bar for that matter. He doesn't know why everyone looks. It might be a survival reflex. He is not sure. Maybe beer and whiskey brings that out in a man. He doesn't know. He doesn't care. The man entering is a fairly good looking man. He is dressed decently in jeans and a golf shirt and loafers. You don't see loafers much these days. He never liked loafers. Maybe it was their name he didn't like. Everyone but the drunk turns back to their drinking.

The new man has drawn his attention for some reason. He doesn't know why. He thinks that there is nothing special about this guy except maybe the loafers he is wearing. He is wearing loafers with no socks. What a weirdo. Feet get so sweaty with no socks. He must be nuts; or really really cool.

The barfly thinks, *there is nothing special about the man so what is it about him? It is just a new face in an old local bar? Yeh, that is probably it.*

He is walking slowly looking for a seat at the bar. He is getting nearer and nearer to the drunk. His chest begins to expand.

He is just coming up closer to him. The drunk is just taking the last little bit from his glass when his hearing begins to fade. He stops his drinking and looks around to see if anyone else is having difficulty with their hearing. Apparently not. Everyone is carrying on as they always do. They are laughing, telling jokes and smiling. Just drinking like him. Then his hearing completely escapes him. He immediately hears a slurping sound; a sound of a straw sucking up the last of the liquid in the bottom of a can. It ends with an echoing empty hollow sound. He looks up at the mirror in front of him behind the bar. He looks into his blank empty eyes. They look back at him as if they are the eyes of a dead man.

Ironically, the eyes looking back at him look like pretty much the same eyes he had been seeing for years only deader; absolutely now life. Not a glimmer or spark of life is in those eyes. They look like the eyes of those soldiers who were shot and died next to him on the battlefield in that stupid war our government got us into. The same dead lifeless eyes. Vacant. Empty. A dead man's eyes.

CHAPTER TWELVE

Lute and Matt awaken to another beautiful morning. The sun is up and a few clouds are dotting the sky. The morning temperature is perfect as will be the rest of the day. Breakfast is yummy and filling. They each take their coffee mugs, jump into the car and head east. The destination is the rebuilt church outside of town. Lute tells Matt more about the church saying, "It had burned down under suspicious circumstances, the paper had said. The fire department suspected arson but could not quit prove it. So the insurance company finally, after years of haggling, paid off on the claim."

"The rumor mill had it that a group of religious zealots had claimed that the church was not a Christian church at all but a coven of witches. This of course proved false because we all know that there are no such things as witches. The stigma lingers to this day, though."

Matt asks, "Who rebuilt it? Are they the tenets?

Lute replied, "I don't know. Let's go down to the Court House and have a look see at the deeds. If that doesn't work we can go visit the Trident Real Estate office.

Lute turns the car around and heads for the Court House.

It is an old granite structure in the style of the 20s and 30s. It has huge pillars holding up the triangular facade that says "Essex County Court House" in Roman letters. It is very impressive.

The two of them march up the bazillion or so steps and through the large doors.

The highly polished marble floor is so shiny that Matt can see his face in it.

The sign on the wall says that the Office of Deeds and Records was on the second floor, Room 202.

After pantingly trekking up the marble steps while holding on to the oak handrail they enter Room 202.

In front of them is a chest high oak counter with a 3/8ths thick piece of glass protecting the beautiful surface.

Lute marches over to it, leans on it and asks the clerk about the church.

"What church is that?" replies the clerk.

Lute and Matt look at each other. Lute sighs. He is a bit disappointed in himself for not having found out the name of the church; let alone learning the address.

Luther said, "You know that rebuilt one that is out of town a bit."

The clerk nods, grabs hold of his checkered ties and straightens it. He goes to his desk and grabs a phone book. He returns to the counter with the book.

"Let's see. What is the name of that church?" He mumbles a bit.

He calls over his shoulder to his colleague asking, "What is the name of that church that burned down and just got rebuilt in the last few years?"

The colleague thinks about it. He draws a blank.

The clerk says, "Golly guys, I just cannot think of it. I wish I was more help."

Lute says, "Hey, don't sweat it. We'll just mosey on out there and get the information. Thanks for the effort."

Luther and Matthew wave their good byes and leave.

Instead of heading to the church they decide to go the Trident Real Estate Office, which is next to the convenience grocery store.

Lute asks, "Do you remember Miss Setaan?"

"I remember her from when were kids. She was older than us but still really pretty. I also remember that she was a popular girl. She was a hit with all the guys. God had put her together rather well."

"Yes! Yes! I remember that. Oh, I remember about her now."

"Oh, that is right. I remember that now. Wonder where she went?"

They got to the real estate office in relative silence. Each is absorbed in his memories of that dead man and his uttering Anima.

They pull up to the glass fronted building. It has a great location on the main drag. It is landscaped with elderberry bushes and decorative grasses surrounded by river stone.

The glass entrance door is pulled outward and they enter a pleasantly A/C'd room. A row of paneled office doors line the far wall. A receptionist manned the front desk.

She has red hair cut in a page boy manner. It is cute on her because it goes perfectly with her large green eyes, high cheek bones and large lips. One could think of her as a cute doll. She has an orange, silk, long-sleeved blouse buttoned to the neck.

She pleasantly asks, "May I be of assistance?" Luther has always thought that that phraseology is so idiotic. *Of course you can. Otherwise I would not have come through the door.* Better to say, *How may I assist you?* Luther always was a stickler.

"Yes", Matt hurriedly said before Lute can go in to a diatribe. It works.

"We are Matthew Thomas and Luther St. Johns. We are here to see Setaan."

The red headed receptionist smiles, picks up the phone and dials a few numbers. A low ringing can be heard coming from one of the offices down on the right, perhaps the one on the end.

The receptionist says into the mouth piece, "Setaan, there are two gentlemen here to see you. Yes. That will fine." She hangs up.

She smiles showing her beautiful teeth and says, "Setaan will be out for you in a moment. She is on a phone call. Please, have a seat over there."

"Over there" is along the front glass window where a few chairs are randomly placed around a table with magazines on it.

Lute picks up a mag and browses. Matt sits and thinks. He tends to do that when there is a puzzle surrounding his life.

Shortly, the door to the end office opens and an attractive older woman comes out, heading toward them. She rounds the ficus tree, apparently still a popular indoor decoration.

She is dressed in a stylish gray business suit with a ruffled white blouse. Her wavy blond hair is accented with three quarter caret diamond ear rings. In a word-she is striking-standing in her two-inch black heels. And yes, she is still all woman as the she had been all though years ago when they were eleven.

She stands in front of them and extends her hand as they stand up. They each shake hands and introduce themselves.

"Well, what can I do for the two of you gentlemen?" Setaan asks.

Luther starts out slowly saying, "You, um, undoubtedly don't know or, um, remember us. We knew you when we were ten or eleven. You were older than us, obviously."

"Yes, you are right. I do not remember you."

"Well, there was a third one of us; Digger, the undertaker and physician."

Setaan hesitates before answering, "I remember something of the three of you. What was it? I can't remember."

Matthew says, "We were the three who found that dead man next to the tracks way back then. You remember? It was in the paper."

She slowly responds, "It's coming back to me. Come with me to my office."

She says, "Thank you, Heidi." The red head nods and goes back to her duties.

Setaan leads the way to her office.

Her office is Spartan. One picture of what looks like a monastery on the wall behind the glass-topped desk, two three-drawer file cabinets behind the desk, her chair and two others for clients to sit in completed the room.

Each sits down. She stares over her desk at them. She then says, "So you are two of the three who found that poor man. That must have very traumatic for you three, being such young ones.

"I was sorry to hear about Digger. He was a good man. I knew of him. I had never met him."

"I remember not seeing you around anymore shortly after we found that guy," Luther said.

"Yes. I moved away."

"Miss Setaan, you were the school counselor back then." Matthew says.

Luther continues, "We were to have one on ones with you about our experience with the dead man. I guess that was what we were going to do with you. You were going to make our minds cope with the incident."

Matthew and Luther look at each other. Their minds are traveling back to their junior high days when Miss Setaan was that most voluptuous woman they had ever seen. And they were going to be in the same room with her by themselves, and with the door closed. Talk about heaven on earth.

Being with her and being so close to her was all the boys could talk about for days and days when they were younger.

They obviously were looking forward to their meetings, but they never happened. Miss Setaan moved away somewhere. They missed out on all of that wonderfulness being so close to them and talking with them.

"When did you move back?" Luther asks.

"Two or three years ago," she says. "Did anyone talk with you about the event?"

Luther says, "Yeh. Some old retired guy talked to us."

Luther looks over at Matthew. Matthew returns the look. They both shake their heads, remembering their disappointment at missing out on Miss Setaan. Miss Setaan was replaced by some wrinkled guy.

Setaan says, "That was Mr. Howard. He retired from that position. It was I who replaced him. Did he do well for you? I mean, were your minds eased?"

Matthew and Luther nod their heads to her. They turn to each other and stare.

There was one thing that they never discussed with Mr. Howard or anyone; just among themselves.

They never mentioned the dying exclamation, Anima that came out with that man's last gasp.

Neither can say why the three kept it to themselves. Maybe because they had never heard of that type thing happening to anyone. They did not want people to talk about them being crazy or stupid.

She breaks their memory laning, "I never realized that Digger was one of the three who found him."

Luther replies, "Yeh. That is when he began thinking of doing something medical."

"As I said, he was a good man. I wish I had actually met him." She then asks, "What is it that I can do for you two?"

"Well," Matthew said, "We are interested in that church."

She sits up a little straighter and asks, "What church is that?"

"The one that was rebuilt two or three years ago. You might remember or know that it burned down years ago and someone has rebuilt it."

She hesitates, and then says, "Yes, I do know the church."

Luther says, "We've been wondering about it. What is its name?"

She slowly says, "THE CHURCH FOR SOULS."

"That is an interesting name. How did it get that name?" Matt asks.

She says, "From what I understand the church is in the soul business. Aren't churches supposed to be in the soul business?"

"Well, yes of course. The soul is the purpose of our living. Without it we are dead."

She slightly smiles at that and says, "How very true."

Matt asks, "Who owns it?"

"Who owns it?" she asks. "I don't know who actually owns it."

She abruptly says, "Well, gentlemen, it has certainly been enjoyable and enlightening. Please stop whenever you believe that I can be of further service. Good day."

They say their thanks and good byes and turn to leave.

"Oh, by the way, one more thing. Was there anything else happening when you found that dead man?" she asks.

Matt immediately says, "No" before Luther can say a thing.

They leave.

CHAPTER THIRTEEN

A man and a woman, husband and wife, Clarence and Matilda are eating at the breakfast table. Matilda is reading the paper ignoring Clarence.

They are each dressed to meet the day; he in his tan summer business suit and she in a summery lime green dress.

Clarence is asking her, "Matilda, what do you have going today?"

Silence.

"Sweetheart," he tries again.

Silence.

"Would you like some more coffee?"

Silence.

"Toast?"

Silence.

"I was thinking perhaps we could head to the park this Saturday and have a picnic. And I can paddle you around in a boat on the lake like we used to, back in the day."

Silence.

That evening there is more of the same as the morning.

Clarence comes through the front door home from work. Matilda, of course does not greet him. She hasn't met him at the door since... Well he can't remember when.

He calls out, "Matilda. I'm home, darling."

He can hear her in the bedroom talking to someone. Oh, she is on the phone talking to someone. Probably her girlfriend.

He crosses the living room, moves on down the hall, raps on the bedroom door, opens it, standing in the doorway.

He hears clearly now this half of the conversation. She is saying, "... Yes, of course I will. You know you can count on me. I am faithful as a beagle."

Pause.

Then, "Norma, I said that I will be there and I will. I have nothing else to do Saturday. Nothing at all." She says this as she looks directly at Clarence.

Clarence backs out of the doorway and gently closes the door. He slowly walks down the hallway to the kitchen.

He grabs a rocks glass, pours a stiff bourbon, adds ice and goes out onto the back patio.

His thoughts wander back to the days; the days that he and Matilda had fallen love and had gotten married. It was a glorious time of their lives.

He and Matilda were so happy together. They did everything together; grocery shopping, movies, taking strolls through the neighborhood in the evenings, getting the car's oil changed, virtually everything.

And their lovemaking was for the record books. It was beyond fantastic. Each of their wants and desires were taken care of; lovingly and caringly.

Ah, the good old days.

Then there was their one and only child. She was fortunate to have made it in the first place. There were complications, both Matilda and their daughter, Susan, almost didn't make it.

But they did, though, thank God. The down side of it was the Matilda was unable to have more children. That was okay. They had little Susie.

Susie's presence added even more joy and love to their happy home. She was growing up as any child does.

She was happy and very much loved.

Then tragedy struck. No one could have foreseen it. Who could know that a tiny little mosquito could carry such a wallop? But it did.

At first, Susie was just a little tired. That happens sometimes. Kids get tired, right? But then she became very tired and did not want to move. She began running a fever; not a big one but enough to give her two baby aspirins and put her to bed early.

They knew that the flu was going around the school and would soon pass. We had gone through this before. We were not too worried.

In the middle of the night Susie began to moan. We both went in to care for her. She was sweating up a storm.

They gave her two more baby aspirins.

They removed her pajamas and sponged-bathed her to help cool her down. Her temperature was higher but not higher than it has been in the past.

They re-pj'd her, kissed her and nestled her back into bed. They turned off the light, closed the door and we went back to bed.

In the morning we knew that there was something drastically wrong with Susan. Maybe this was not the flu; her temperature was two degrees higher than ever before. She was listless groggy. Her neck was stiff.

They took her to the emergency room. They looked at her, took her temperature and whisked her away just as a convulsion began.

That was the last time...

When they saw her next, she was sleeping. She never woke up.

Susan died two days later of encephalitis. Not only did our Susan die, so did their marriage.

Clarence finished his drink. He made a sandwich for dinner and ate in the solitude of the kitchen.

Matilda never came out of the bedroom all evening.

At bed time Clarence crawls into the bed beside his wife. He is feeling a bit frisky as people do after so long a time.

He sidles up to her from behind and puts his right arm amorously around his wife's waist.

She sits up with a start so quickly that it startles him. She whirls around to face him and sneeringly says through clenched teeth, "Don't you ever dare touch me again. If you even think about it, I will see that you are gelded, you bastard. Now get out of my room!"

Clarence sleeps in the guest room, again.

The next afternoon in the grocery store parking lot, as Matilda is loading up the car with groceries which she had just purchased, she notices that the traffic noise on the highway was fading away. And then the noise was entirely gone. She immediately hears a slurping sound; a sound as if a straw is sucking the last of liquid from the bottom of a can. It ends with an echoing empty hollow sound.

She looks up and sees a rather nice looking older women walking past her car toward the real estate office which is next to the store.

She gets into her car, looks in the rear view mirror and sees, staring back her, her empty lifeless eyes; the eyes of a dead person.

That evening after work, Clarence does not go home. Instead, he heads to a restaurant/bar, The Fiery Pit. He has never been to it but he has heard good things about it. And sure enough the good things he has heard are true.

It is not long before a pretty older blond comes into the bar area. She sits a few seats down from him. It is Setaan.

She orders a Manhattan, up with three dashes of bitters. Before she can say put it on a tab, Clarence, like a knight in shining armor, calls over to the bartender, "Her tab is on mine tonight."

That is the beginning.

They have one more drink, she a Manhattan, he a bourbon on the rocks at the bar. Then they go into the dining room for dinner.

They get along together famously. It feels good to Clarence to be happy, talkative and laughing.

They each have the ribeye with parsnips and a side salad, along with a few more drinks. Clarence pays the tab and escorts her out the door.

They chit-chat on the way to their cars which just happen to be parked next to one another.

Clarence says, "I'm not quit tired yet. How about you?"

"No. I'm not either."

He ventures, "Let's say we get a motel room for a while."

"That will be wonderful, Clarence. I was hoping you would say that. If you hadn't, I believe that I would have asked you."

They decided to drive their own cars for convenience purposes.

He gets into his gray Jeep Patriot. She gets into her black Cadillac SUV with the Trident Real Estate magnetized sign on the door.

Upon opening the door to the room with the pass key, they immediately embrace like two newlyweds on their first night ever. She tears at his clothes. He tears at hers. Even before they are fully disrobed they are on the bed making passionate love.

This love making is repeated three times throughout the night.

When dawn begins, the girl quietly dresses, kisses him good day.

She dangerously lies down next to him. He hugs her one more time while they kiss. Her chest expands as if inhaling.

Then the oddest thing happens. Clarence's hearing begins to fade. When it is completely silent, he hears a slurping sound; a sound of a straw sucking the last of liquid from the bottom of a can. It ends with an echoing hollow sound.

When she leaves, she blows him a kiss, thanks for for everything and closes the door.

Clarence arises and goes into the bathroom and sees lifeless empty eyes staring back at him. They are as if dead.

He cries.

CHAPTER FOURTEEN

Matt and Lute return to the County Court House and enter the Office of Deeds.

As they walk into the office, the clerk sees them and calls out from his desk, "THE CHURCH OF SOULS." Matthew and Luther agree nodding their heads.

The three meet together at the counter. He is carrying a tome of what turns out to be listings of deeds for the county going back twenty years. The clerk opens the book to an already marked page, runs his finger down the column until it reaches THE CHURCH FOR SOULS entry.

Running his finger from left to right he reads out loud:

> THE CHURCH FOR SOULS
> 6660 Dam Lane
> Salem MA 01970
> Structure: Wooden church building
> Purpose: Gather in souls
> Owner: Universal Soul Gatherers LLC
> Status: Not for profit; tax exempt; members not liable

The clerk continues to say that THE CHURCH FOR SOULS began meeting in that building almost three years ago.

Very interesting, Matt thinks to himself. He wonders if Lute has picked up on it. He probably has. He is pretty quick, sometimes.

Lute thanks the clerk, they say their good-byes, again and return to the car. He turns the engine on, turns on the A/C and rolls down the windows. It is hot.

While the A/C is trying to do its thing, the two of them are lost in their own thoughts.

Lute rolls up the windows when the car temperature feels suitable for being comfortable.

Matt breaks the silence. "Lute, did you pick up on that?"

"Yes."

Matt said, "The soup is beginning to thicken. When we were talking with Setaan, she seemed to do some squirming and hemming and hawing. She changed the subject real quick when you asked her how long she had been back. Did you notice?"

"Yes I did. She seemed to be more than interested in our finding that guy and if there was anything else that went on, other than finding it."

"Yes, I am getting the feeling that whatever is going on with these people Animaing all over the place, Setaan knows more than she is saying. And that name, Setaan, is quite unusual would you agree?"

"Yes it is. I thought so at the time, also."

"Any theories?"

Matt replies, "I have one beginning to form.

"Let's hear it."

Matt begins with, "Let's review all that we know."

He begins to count on his fingers:

1. Anima is being gasped from people on their last breath
2. Digger was being followed
3. The black church vehicle was seen leaving Digger's accident
4. THE CHURCH FOR SOULS rebuilt and opened almost three years ago

5. About the same time Digger began to hear Anima like we had heard all those years ago

6. Setaan (strange name) seems to be aware or is involved with whatever this is

7. The church is in the soul business- Anima means soul

They mull over the known list in their minds. *Cogitating is good for the soul*, Matt always says.

Lute drives away toward 6660 Dam Lane.

CHAPTER FIFTEEN

Heading toward THE CHURCH FOR SOULS, they drive past the PITT MANUFACTURING COMPANY. This company has been in town since the 30's. It was sold to one of the employees thirty years later. That employee ran it successfully for five years. Then suddenly he died, leaving a wife and a young son.

The wife remarried a divorced man with a son three years older than her.

Her son, Boris Pitt, is now working for the company. He manages the office overseeing the goings on of the secretaries and the scheduler all the while being the purchasing department. He took over the purchasing duties from his step-brother three months earlier.

He does a competent enough job. However, his step father does not appreciate or care much for the young man who has married his precious princess.

His princess, Margrethe, remained with and grew up with her mom. They moved to Manchester by the Sea soon after the divorce. They had a cozy home on Norton's Point Road overlooking the bay, where they can keep on eye on their sailboat.

Margrethe grew up sailing the bay and ocean since the age of eight. She is an accomplished captain having won many regatta races. This, as it turns out, appeals to Boris because he also sails.

They have known each other since childhood. Boris and Margarethe would occasionally meet at family get-togethers. They always enjoyed each other's company. And as they got older their friendship blossomed into love.

They attended the same university all four years. Upon graduation they eloped, which angered Margarethe's father greatly. He has never forgiven his step son for taking away his princess.

At the plant there is as little communication between the step son and step-father as possible; just enough to maintain the plant operations. The employees are not aware of any friction between the two. It is family business, which is not to be aired in public.

Now, at family gatherings, the step son stays pretty much to himself. His wife enjoys the get-togethers and does not pay very close attention to her husband. Occasionally there will be a, 'Hows it going?' Or, 'Is everything alright?' He will dutifully answer with, 'I'm doing fine.' And, 'yes'.

When there are games to be played such as croquet, the step-father and step-brother gang up on him. He inevitably loses. His wife does not seem to notice. Perhaps she doesn't. He does not know nor does he care to ask her. He will keep his growing misery to himself.

During contract negotiating season with the transportation firms, Boris is not pleased with the existing contracts terms his step brother has negotiated.

He vows to himself that he will play hardball this year and get a better deal for the company. He is in the driver's seat and he is going to use that power for all it is worth.

Speaking of worth, the transportation costs are close to $2.5 million.

His goal is a 10% reduction in costs or $250,000. He would start out at 15% or $375,000.

When the dust settles, he reached his goal; a 10% reduction in costs per year for the next three years.

He announces his success to his step-father and step-brother the cost savings in transportation cost over the next three years of $750,000. He is proud of his achievement. And he wants to rub his step-brother's nose in it a bit; showing his step-father his value.

He does not receive much of an "atta boy" as he had hoped for. But not being deterred from his quest which is, "Step Father, I would like to share in this wind-fall. I would like, as a bonus, 10% of the first year's savings spread over the three contract period. That will be $25,000 or $8,333 per year."

The step-father stares at him. Finally after sometime of silence and staring, the step-father says, "I will see what I can do."

That is it. That is the end of it. There is no more. In fact, a year goes by and he hears or receives nothing.

However, something that does change is that he begins complaining to his friends. Boris begins grousing. a grumble here and there. Nothing definite, vague crabs. Nothing that the fellow workers notice. The step-father certainly does not.

Soon enough though, Boris tells them about all of the nasty unkind things that has gone on down through the years.

As time wears on, he becomes very demonstrative in his criticisms. He begins referring to his step father as the Old Man.

His wife is aware of the dislike her father has for her husband. But she is not aware of the destruction it is wreaking on him.

Boris' health begins to go downhill. He is drinking more and not sleeping very well. His anger has turned to hatred. It is eating him up inside. This type of living is not healthy

One day he is summoned into his step-father office. There is a salesman talking with the old man. The salesman wants to meet Boris before he leaves for his next appointment. He introduces himself to the step-son.

During the handshake the salesman's chest expands as if inhaling. Boris' hearing begins to fade. When there is complete silence he immediately hears a slurping sound; the sound of a straw sucking up the last of the liquid in an empty can. It ends with an echoing hollow sound.

The salesman sees the eyes go blank empty as if dead.

The man turns and shakes the hand of the old man. The step-father's hearing begins to fade. The man's chest enlarges as if inhaling. When there was complete silence he, he immediately hears a slurping sound; the sound of a straw sucking up the remains of a liquid in the bottom of a can. It ends with an echoing hollow sound.

The salesman sees the eyes go blank, empty, as if dead.

He smiles.

He leaves.

CHAPTER SIXTEEN

They continue heading northwest out of town toward THE CHURCH FOR SOULS. The houses thin as they near the town's limit. This is different from Las Vegas, where the houses are dense up to the point of no more building.

The church they know is about three miles from town. It is in a sort of woods. It is far enough off the road that it cannot be seen from the road so they need to be on their toes so as to not miss it.

They approach the road the church is on. They know this because they just passed the broken down 1947 Ford pickup on the right that they were told about is a landmark.

They turn right onto the dirt road named Dam Lane. There, after another right turn and continuing straight ahead, is THE CHURCH FOR THE SOULS.

They were astonished at what they saw.

The wooden church is painted a flat black with glossy red window trim.

"Oh! My! God," cries Lute! "Have you ever seen such a thing?"

"No."

They slowly drive past it, staring as they go.

The thing has a spire and curved pointed windows like older wooden churches have. The ten-inch wide boards are placed vertically, giving the church the illusion of being taller.

The front double-doors are at least twelve feet high. The doors are painted the glossy red, also.

Above them is seen the name- THE CHURCH FOR SOULS in Times New Roman font. The letters are black with a red rectangle background.

Lute pulls to the curb. The two of them just sit there in silence. Neither has seen such a sight. It is unheard of to have a black church building. Black denotes darkness, not light; a hole, not sky. It shows evil.

The glossy bright red window frames are quite the contrast to the flat black building, really stand out.

It is a large building that can easily hold two hundred congregates.

The kicker of the entire site-if one can consider a black church building to be able to be topped-is the more than huge stained glass windows. They are the biggest windows either of them had ever seen.

Not a pastoral scene is to be seen. No human figures, no angels, none of the windows show panoramas that other churches have.

What is seen is a picture of an active volcano with smoke, ash and flowing lava. Another window is filled with flames. Another shows the devastation of a battle field; destruction everywhere. The last window shows a cemetery with crypts and grave stones.

Matt says, "Let's go have a peek."

"K."

They both get out, and for some reason, they quietly close their doors; no slamming.

They notice that the lawn is beautifully kempt. The bushes are also kept very tidy.

They walk up the seven steps and try the door. It is locked.

Lute knocks; not with much conviction.

Matt pounds the door with the balled-up side of his hand.

They wait. No answer. They hear no movement inside.

Matt pounds again. Again, no answer.

Matt shrugs and says, "Let us walk around to if there is anything else to see.

They retrace their steps down and walk to the right side of the building.

Matt leads opting for the right side; from habit and experience. When visiting any amusement parks, fairs and carnivals always go the right. There is less traffic in that direction; especially in the morning. The large majority, upon entering these places, immediately go left.

Lute looks at the first stained window. He immediately knows that this is a very well made window.

"Matt, notice the thickness of the weld holding the pieces of glass together. See the different colors that are found on each individual piece. It is beautiful craftsmanship. No wonder they have a thick piece of plexi-glass protecting it from harm."

They move to the next window. Once again Lute remarks, "This is beautiful."

They walk around the back and see a windowless steel door. This is also locked.

There are no windows on the back side.

They walked around to the other side. These two windows are protected the same as the other two.

None of the four can be opened nor can inquiring eyes peer in.

Lute notices that there are four tubes counter sunk into the ground in front of each window. *Huh?*

Matt checks out the roof; there are no communication dishes of any kind. No wires are seen going into the building. Either they have no electricity or the wires are underground.

"There is no one around and we cannot get into the building, I guess we are coming up short," says Lute.

"It is not a complete waste of time. When was the last time you saw a black painted church with red window trim?'" asks Matt?

They reluctantly return to the car and drive back home.

CHAPTER SEVENTEEN

As Lute and Matt head up to the front door of Lute's home, Matt picks up the newspaper laying on the porch. It is the town's attempt at keeping the community informed about the goings-on within the county.

Matt has not seen the local paper for decades. He is interested in giving it a gander to see if he can notice differences from then to now.

He moseys into the kitchen to make himself a drink and grab a beer for Lute. He does both and goes to the living room where he hands over the beer and plops himself down in the easy chair in the corner, opposite the kitchen.

He takes a sip and looks at the front page of the paper. The banner is the same. The font is the same as far as he can remember. The columns and the spacing seem the same, also.

Well, that feels good. Who says that you cannot go home? Not everything changes.

He reads the front page and follows the *continued on the next page* with little interest, until he comes to the Community Interests page. The top of the page reads, *AREA PHILANTHROPIST DONATES.*

He scans down the first column and sees that the story is about a friend of his and Lute's.

"Hey Lute," he calls out, "Here is a story about Ivan T. Thornbush . You remember him don't you?"

"Yep. He is that rich kid; lived over there on Thornbush. His family always thought that they were a big deal. As if they earned all that money instead of it being handed down from their great-grandfather. All they ever did was live off the interest."

"Ivan never did work a day in his life. He was and still is a stuck-up snob." Lute continues. "I don't get it. The whole town thinks he is God's gift to us. How come the people don't see him for what he is; a hypocrite?"

Matt says, "Here, let me read this piece. Maybe it will shed some light on him."

Matt reads,

> *Our town of Salem is very proud of one of its own. Ivan T. Thornbush is this year's recipient of the prestigious "Salem Pride Award" for being an outstanding example of what it means to be a great asset to the community.*
>
> *Past recipients have been judges, Senators, Doctors, Nobel Prize winners, and now this year's philanthropist extraordinaire: Ivan T. Thornbush.*
>
> *Ivan is known throughout the county as being a most generous man. Whether the cause is personal or community motivated, Ivan T. Thornbush is the "go to" guy.*
>
> *Looking back over his past generosities, one can notice a pattern in his helping aid.*
>
> *When it affects children, Ivan is in the forefront fighting for and directing the efforts in each cause. These things include a new wing on the library dedicated to children's themes, playground equipment at the elementary school, sledding hill for winter fun at North Park; to name a few causes he has spearheaded and generously donated to over the years.*
>
> *Of course, these each bear his name, which is only right, since he has been so instrumental in their creation. He humbly accepted the City Father's insistence of the inclusion of his name at these sites.*

Ivan T. Thornbush is known for his philanthropy to the Salem Arts Center assisting in the funding for the theater renovation. He has also given to the American Red Cross and the Salvation Army (for both of these he was honored last year).

He aids the American Boy Scouts, Girl Scouts, Cub Scouts and Indian Guides. He gives generously to his church; in which he is the head deacon.

The list can go on and on. Needless to say, this is a great great man for our community of Salem, Massachusetts.

Matt says, Wow! This is quite the fellow."

Lute replies, "This is exactly what I was saying. The town is gaga over this fraud. He is a Hypocrite with a capital H."

"I do not understand."

"Look, "Lute says, "Ivan Thornbush is no more interested in any of these causes other than to get his name be emblazoned on each."

"Lute, "Where is this coming from?"

"Look Matt, a few years ago I was at a shin dig out at his place. I don't remember what it was for."

"Well, anyway, I needed to lie down to take a load off; I was getting one of those head aches and I wanted to stave it off if I could. I wandered around the place's 50,000 or so rooms until I found one that was far enough away that I could not hear the party noise.

"I walked across the three acre carpet and laid down on the sofa that was facing the fire place. The fire was not burning."

"I was in there no more than five minutes before the door opened letting two voices into the room. The door closed."

"I heard footsteps and the voices go to the bureau. There, apparently, is where glasses and alcohol are kept."

"I hear Ivan ask, 'Hey, Heinrich, what are you drinking?'"

"Heinrich replies, 'Scotch, what else is there?'"

"'Right you are,' said Ivan'"

"The drinks were poured and I hear them sit in chairs near the bureau."

"They sat for a moment sipping. I could hear the ice clinking."

"Then Heinrich says, 'This is quite the honorable thing you have done for the town.'"

"Town Shmown. The people in this town are shmucks. No one in our college fraternity would have been allowed any of these town's people to join. They are all nothings."

"They think I do all these things for them. BS. I do it for me. Have you noticed, my named is chiseled all over the town? Hell, I wouldn't be surprised if they don't rename this little burg's to honor me.

"Just imagine, Ivansville, Ivansburg. Or, hey, how about Thornbushville, Massachusetts? Oh yeh, I do like that one."

"Yeh, that does have a nice ring to it."

"These people have no idea of how little taxes I pay to our beloved government. Almost nothing. Hell, what I don't pay in taxes I give to the city and get my named immortalized. Pretty cool, huh?"

"The town loves me. Aannd it feeels reeally good! Ha ha ha!"

"Hey Heinrich, drink up. I have to get back to this piece of crap party."

Lute then says, "Well. How do you like him now?"

"You are right. He is quite the schmuck. And the town's people are a bunch of sycophants."

At this same time Ivan is out in the bay off of Long Point. He is a comfortable mile off shore. There is not much traffic on the water at this hour; most are at home having supper.

Not Ivan. He is entertaining on his 70-foot yacht named *Witch*. The twenty or so guests are mingling among each other enjoying the gentle off shore breeze. This makes for a smooth non-healing evening cruise.

Ivan is at the helm while the hired skipper watches on. The other three hired crew members are manning the lines for the main and jib sails and coiling lines.

The guests are having a whale of a time. They all enjoy the notoriety that accompanies an invitation to cruise on the *Witch*; and the booze is top shelf, of course, and free. When one has more money than God, the best is the only way to go.

For some time now, Ivan has been aware of the smallish sailboat which is also enjoying an evening sail. The boat has been on a near collision course which will allow it to pass on the lee side of the boat.

This is fine. He doesn't have to bother with a sudden luffing of his sails.

He smiles to himself. *Ah. Life is good*, Ivan Thornbush says to himself.

The oncoming boat is getting closer and closer. He waves at the fellow skipper who waves in return.

Suddenly, his hearing begins to disappear. When it is completely gone, he immediately hears a slurping sound; the sound like a straw sucking the last of liquid in the bottom of a can. It ends with an echoing hollow sound.

If any of the revelers had looked at him at that moment they would have seen his eyes grow blank, empty, as like those a dead man.

CHAPTER EIGHTEEN

The next morning finds our two boys having breakfast at Lute's favorite diner, "Jerry's Diner."

Lute has his normal cakes, two sunny side up eggs, rye toast with orange marmalade and coffee, black, please. Matt is continuing his meatless meals having, instead, a two egg omelet with onions and tomatoes and peppers. Yummy.

Matt notices Setaan walking past Jerry's Diner, heading toward town. He quickly stands up, motions with his head at a surprised Lute in the direction of Setaan.

Lute pays as Matt heads out the door and begins walking toward town behind Setaan.

Lute quickly catches up and asks, "What is up?"

"I have no idea. I saw her and got the thought to following her. Nothing more than that."

"Well, this is now beginning to become a Philip Marlow affair. I like this."

They follow at what they consider a safe distance, trying to be inconspicuous. Off in the distance are three young punk-type teens. Sloppy clothes, tattoos, cigarettes, chains hanging from their belts, two have vests on, all three have wife-beaters, engineer boots and the requisite jeans.

These three look as if they are headed to prison at any time. Certainly, they are no asset to the community. It is quite likely that their moms would not care if they never came home again, let alone, if indeed they stopped living at home.

Setaan and the crew are getting closer and closer to one another. It suddenly seems as if there is a lively spring in her step, now. *What is up with that?* Matt thinks.

As the boys come abreast of Setaan, Setaan on the left, the boys on the right, both Matt and Lute watch and see the boys' eyes become empty, like dead men's eyes.

At the same time, Setaan is seen turning her head toward the boys. A reflection is seen in a store front's window of a wry smile creeping across her face and a twinkle in her eyes as she stares right at Matthew and Luther.

Matt and Lute stop in their tracks, watching as the now dead-eyed boys walk past them, unseeingly.

Matt and Lute look at each other. They just stare.

Matt is the first to break the spell. "Now, that was very interesting. Something very important just happened and we saw it. I wonder if we were supposed to see it?"

Lute says, "I bet we were. She looked right at us. And it didn't seem to bother her that we saw what had just happened."

They start walking again in silence.

"Okay. What do we have," Lute asks?

Matt goes over the list and adds the new information:

- Anima is being gasped from people on their last breath
- Digger was being followed
- The black church vehicle was seen leaving Digger's accident
- THE CHURCH FOR SOULS is rebuilt and opened almost three years ago
- The church is in the soul business-Anima means soul
- At about the same time, Digger began hearing Anima like we heard all those years ago as kids
- Setaan seems to be aware of what is happening

- Setaan seems to be involved in this, somehow, someway. We saw her do something to those boys. Whatever she did affected their eyes. They looked like a dead man's eyes
- We did not hear Anima from those boys

Lute said, "Setaan saw us see her. She did not react. She put on that Cheshire smile with a twinkle in her eyes. She walked on with that spring in her step."

"I think she knows that we suspect something and she doesn't seem upset that we might know something."

Lute says, "Let's follow her. I think that is what she wants us to do. I don't think that she would have acted like she did without it being an invitation."

Matt nods his agreement.

They stand in silence; thinking.

Matt breaks the silence, "Lute, if what you think is true, and it sure does seem likely... I think... That we should shadow Setaan."

His momentum is growing and he continues quickly saying, "I think we should stick with her wherever she goes. What day is it?"

Lute says, "Tuesday."

"Ah, Tuesday. The day that is dedicated to John the Baptist. The Greeks say that Tuesday is unlucky. It is also the day of the fall of Constantinople. The Spanish and the Greeks hold that Tuesday the thirteenth is unlucky. While the Thai Solar Calendar has the thirteenth referring to Pali which refers to the "Ashes of the Dead".

"Golly. Thanks Matt. Show off. Thanks for all the help."

"Hey, any little bit helps."

"Okay, so we follow her, then what?"

Matt replies, "We go where she goes; everywhere. All day and into the night, all the way until she goes home.

"And if she sees us watching her?"

"Lute, if what you said is correct and-I think it is-I believe that she will not mind. I believe that this is what she wants.

"And, for whatever her reason, she wants it to be on the QT," Lute puts in.

"Yes. I saw her turn onto, oh what is the name the street that the Trident Real Estate office is on?"

"Red Ash."

"Yeh. Okay, let's head for the car and then on to our first stake out. I am beginning to feel like Philip Marlow, also."

CHAPTER NINETEEN

They drive past the real estate office and see Setaan talking to the red headed Heidi. They were right. They know where she is.

They park in the convenience store parking lot and begin their waiting.

All day passes with Setaan coming to the convenience store for lunch items only.

Matt and Lute take turns going into the store as needed. They even take turns going on short walks within eye sight of the car in case they are needed to return quickly.

Evening comes; closing time is nigh. Setaan is the last to leave. She goes into her Cadillac SUV with the real estate magnet on the side and drives home.

Lute and Matt have purchased enough food and water to carry them through supper and beyond.

Evening comes and goes. Nighttime arrives.

At 11:30, she emerges clothed in a red-hooded robe. The hood is hanging down onto her back. She is carrying a stainless steel bowl, large enough that her right arm needs to be fully extended to carry it. She carries it as if the bowl contained something that might spill.

She places the bowl on the front passenger floor.

She gets into her vehicle and heads out of town.

Lute asks, "Where can she be going at this time of night?"

"We shall find out soon enough. I have an idea from the direction she is going."

Sure enough, the destination is known. She is headed toward THE CHURCH FOR SOULS.

She turns down Dam lane. Lute follows.

They round the bend. In front of them is an unexpected sight. There are hundreds of vehicles parked in neatly defined order.

There all types of vehicles; old beaters to brand new luxury cars.

They have no fear of being noticed in there automobile amongst all of the others. Many of the cars are dark and empty. The others are disgorging their passengers.

To their amazement, each is wearing a red-hooded robe. Some have the hoods on their backs, while others have their hoods over their heads. For those that are wearing them, the hoods prove to be very deep. So deep that the faces inside are completely in shadow; completely unrecognizable.

There is something written on the fronts of the robes but they are too far away to be recognized.

They see Setaan get out of her car and dawn her hood. Hers too is deeply cut. Her face cannot be seen.

She walks across the grass, up the seven steps and enters the church.

Matt and Lute ponder their next move as they watch the assemblage enter the building.

Matt comes up with it, "We need to get in there. We need to see what is going on. We need to find out. If indeed Setaan wanted us to know what is happening, then I believe we are welcome. I believe we have been invited."

"I think you are right. Do you think that we should just walk right on up and in?"

Almost everyone is inside now; no more vehicles are seen arriving. Matt opens his door to get out just as a car's headlights are seen coming down Dam Lane.

It turns out to be a black Rolls Royce limousine. It pulls in front of the church and sits.

The windows are tinted so there is no peeking in. The last of the stragglers disappear through the door. The driver's door opens on the limousine. A man in a red hooded robe gets out of the driver's–side door, moves to the rear door and opens it. A very tall man emerges.

He stands to his full seven feet. He is clad in a shiny black velvet robe with a deep hood attached. He is wearing the hood so that his face is not seen.

He heads to the front doors of the church and begins to climb the stairs.

Just then, Matt opens his door and gets out. Lute continues to follow.

Matt begins to fast walk toward the doors. Lute follows.

The giant shiny black velvet robe stops on the top step, slightly turns his head to the left toward the direction of Matthew and Luther, as if hearing their approach. This furthers his thought that they are welcome and are actually being invited to follow him into THE CHURCH FOR SOULS. The tall man enters the church, disappearing inside through the unclosing doors.

Just before they climb the steps, they both notice that there are multiple torches stuck into the ground in front of the stained glass windows. So that is what those holes were for.

Matt runs up the steps two at a time. Lute follows.

They both enter the building as the doors are closed by two hooded persons. They pay no attention to Luther and Matthew.

It's a relief to the boys, but they wonder why not. It adds fuel to the theory that they have been invited here. That is a comforting thought.

Matt leans over to Lute and whispers, "We are in and it seems as if we are expected. The two at the door did not try to stop us. It is as if we are invited."

"It would seem so."

They now have time to look around. The first thing they notice is that there are no electric lights. What there are instead of incandescents are multiple candles placed in sconces on each of the four walls.

The cathedral ceiling is supported with thick solid cross-beams. The wooden wall and the beams are stained a dark rich brown. Hanging from them are five crystal chandeliers; four smaller ones on the corners of the ceiling, one huge one dangling in the center of the room. There is ample light for sure.

The next thing that hits them is the mass of red-hooded robes surrounded by the flat black walls of the church's interior. They are all facing the front so that their backs are turned toward Matt and Lute.

There is no pulpit, unlike every other church either of them has ever been in. There are pews on either side of a center aisle, as well as aisles between the pews and against the outer walls. There is no adornment on any wall. None.

The stained glass windows are lit by multiple touches outside on the lawn. The flickering fire of the torches adds an eerie-creepy look to the already creepy windows.

The volcano seems to come alive as if it were actually right there. The battle scene window was a somber, sobering look at the horrors of mankind, seeming to vibrate with a life of its own.

The cemetery window is shadowy and misty looking. One does not want to go there at night. And the fire window is the liveliest of the four. The fire picture is lit by flickering touches making for a most remarkable sensation of immensity and depth; it has come alive.

The oddest object in the entire sanctuary is in the front. All eyes focus on it when they are not mesmerized by the windows.

The object is a large vat shaped container appearing to be built into the floor. It appears to be made of stainless steel.

Huh. Stainless like the bowl Setaan carried in with her, thinks Lute

Each hooded figure is grasping onto an identical stainless bowl.

"What is going on?" Lute asks?

"Shh!"

Something was beginning to happen. The big seven foot tall, shiny, black, velvet hood-robed figure has gotten onto the platform behind the vat. He raises his arms and begins to speak.

On the front of his robe is the well-known, six pointe star; known as the Star of David.

Lute leans toward Matt and says, "Look at the symbol on the front of that guy's robe."

Matt looks up and sees a six-point star, the symbol that is on the current flag of Israel.

Matt thinks *this star is considered a very strong symbol of the Jewish people. This symbol was chosen by King Solomon, who is the son of David. However, there is controversy concerning the exact meaning of the symbol.*

Some say that it is actually a Satanist symbol; the hexagram being the symbol that actually refers to Satan, not the Jewish people or Israel.

It is said that the Satanic Illuminist Rothschild of the House of Rothschild in 1896 began funding the plot to regain Israel as a nation. It is he who is credited with insisting the symbol-that the Jews say is the Star of David, which is actually the hexagon of Satan-become the symbol of Israel.

The man up front begins to speak in a language that neither of them has ever heard. To Matt, it seems to be a potpourri of many languages; many old languages that are not even spoken anymore.

All of the hoods stand stock still. They continue to face forward as they listen to the booming voice filling the room.

The black-hooded man is bigger now than what he appeared outside. He still looks over seven feet tall big, but now his massive shoulders are easily seen filling out the robe. This is probably the biggest man either of them has ever seen. The big man should have a booming voice, but what is heard is a rather soft spoken voice; kind and melodic. Such a contrast to what was expected.

Every now and again Matt will catch a word or a phrase; words in classical German, especially, and some in Latin.

Words such as Esser and Geist are familiar to Matt. He tells these to Lute and tells him that they mean 'Eater' and 'Ghost'.

The man in front continues to talk. The red robes remain perfectly still, dutifully holding their bowls. The black robe raises both of his arms and booms out, "FRESSEN!"

Matt leans over to Lute and says, "Fressen means devour."

Lute retorts, "Devours what? Eats what? A ghost?"

Matt shrugs, shakes his head and returns to watching.

The leader calls out a few more words, lowers his hands and bows his head. The red hoods follow suit, bowing.

There is silence.

The black robe moves to his left and sets a long wooden match to a cylinder two inches in diameter. Immediately, black smoke comes forth, rising to the celling.

He moves to his right and lights another cylinder. The large sanctuary will soon have smoke everywhere.

The leader then spreads his arms out away from his sides. His left hand is formed in the Devil's Triad, the Satanic Salute. This is made by pointing the first and fifth fingers while curling the thumb and third and fourth fingers to the palm.

He calls out in a sweet voice, "Geist Essers come forth. Bring your Animas."

It now becomes clear to Matt. He does not know it all but he knows the gist of what this was about.

He leans to Lute and whispers to him, "These people in the red robes take souls. Or more specifically, they go around collecting souls. They are called Geist Essers; Soul Eaters."

Lute just stares at him.

Just then, a processional of the Geist Essers begins to slowly move up to the vat and, thicker gooey, ivory-colored oozes into the vat. Their left arms are thrust upward with their hand in the Devil's Triad symbol.

Both Matt and Lute lean over to look inside of a bowl as it is carried down the center aisle. What they see is a thick, silvery gray goo; with a very high viscosity. It has the consistency of a heavy cream sauce. There is a slight glow as if the bowl was filled with luciferins

With each pouring, the leader calls out in his melodic voice, "ANIMA." The two hundred red robes echo him with, "Anima."

Both Matt and Lute look at each other and mouth the word, "soul."

Lute almost screams out, "The bowls hold souls. They are pouring souls into the vat! OH! MY! GOD!"

They both stare wide-eyed at the spectacle. Someone sidles up to the side of Matthew. He looks over, seeing Setaan. She moves in front of both Matthew and Luther.

There, on the front of her robe, is the Leviathan Cross. This symbol looks like an infinity sign with a double-barred cross stuck into it.

Matt says to Lute, "That symbol can mean Hail Satan. It is said to be a very powerful symbol. It can destroy one's enemies. Others say that it is the sign of free choice."

"Each of us has this symbol on our robes," Setaan says.

"I can see that."

"Our leader, the one up front in the shiny black robe, restarted here after we rebuilt the church. He is known as Seele Fresser, Soul Devourer. "He is the one who got this church rebuilt. He is one who put out the call to the Geist Essers worldwide announcing the reopening of the Salem Massachusetts' chapter of THE CHURCH FOR SOULS."

Matt's eyes widen as he begins to better understand what is happening.

Setaan notices and says, "Yes, there are human souls in these bowls. We have been harvesting this batch since last Tuesday the thirteenth."

"Harvest? What do you mean harvesting souls? How do you harvest them?" asks Luther.

"Tomorrow," Setaan quietly says.

"What! Tomorrow? What do you mean, tomorrow?" exasperatingly retorts Luther.

"Let us meet for breakfast tomorrow. I will tell you both more of what is happening in the whole world."

Luther replies, "Yes of course. Where?"

"At Jerry's Diner. I saw the two of you eating there. Sound good?"

"Yeh that will be great. See you there at nine?"

"Until then."

She pivots on her feet and walks toward the back of the church. Matt and Lute stand in place stare at her receding figure. They look at each other.

Matt says, "Oh my gosh. This is getting creepier and creepier. She just said they harvest souls."

"What does that mean, exactly?" asks Lute?

"I do not know."

"Souls are in the bowls? What is going on? How can this be? I thought that God took care of all the souls? What are these people doing with them?"

The event continues for hours. The boys stay in the church watching the non-stop procession of Geist Essers chanting, processing up to the big abyss and dumping their stainless steel bowls down into wherever the opening goes, all the while chanting "Anima." Creepy.

Finally, the time and the smoke drive them out into the torch lit night. The stars in the sky are shining. The trees are gently swaying.

They slowly walk to Lute's car. When they get to it, they turn to look at the eerie, shiny, black church with the red doors. The torches add the touch of unearthliness, making it seem to come alive.

CHAPTER TWENTY

The boys head home to Lute's house. Lute immediately heads to the refridge and grabs a beer, opens it, and takes a big swig. Matt heads for the cupboard, which houses the scotch. He pours a hefty one, takes a large drink, refills it and throws some ice cubes into the glass.

They go to the living room. Lute hits the sofa, Matt the lounge chair. Neither says a word. They are absorbed in their own thoughts about the evening. Well, not evening. It is 5:30 in the morning.

They sip in silence for about ten minutes. Matt gets up, goes to the kitchen, refills his rocks glass, grabs a beer for Lute, returns to the living room, hands Lute the beer, returns to his chair and sits.

Matt breaks the silence, saying, "Anima means soul. The bowls were full of souls. Dying people were gasping the word Anima with their last breath. Setaan says that the soul harvesting is happening all around the world. The Geist Essers are chanting Anima as they slowly march down the center aisle of the church, pouring the thick oyster colored liquid mass down the hole.

"Lute, we are learning a lot more but I cannot put it all together. Can you?"

"No."

More silence enters the room.

They each finish their drinks and shuffle off to their individual bed rooms. Nine o'clock is going to arrive very soon. They are going to need as much sleep as possible. Even so, they will still be very tired.

CHAPTER TWENTY ONE

They sleep until eight thirty. They dress in casual shorts and golf shirts and head for Jerry's Setaan is already there when Matt and Lute enter the diner at the appointed time. Setaan has secured a booth in the back end of the long diner.

She is wearing a comfortable yellow shift with baseball sized white flowers polka dotting the material. Sha has white leather flats on her feet.

She says, "I arrived a bit early knowing that this place fills up quickly and stays filled." She says this as she takes a sip of coffee.

Lute and Matt slide into the booth opposite Setaan.

An efficient waitress sidles over from the next booth and takes their coffee orders. Matt tells the waitress that the check goes to him.

Setaan asks how long they stayed last night. When Lute tells her, she says that they look in pretty good shape, considering the very little sleep they got. Lute tells her that he suspects that that is due to the excitement of the evening and the anticipation of this breakfast with her.

The coffee arrives. They each place their breakfast order with the waitress; Setaan asks for French toast with crispy bacon and a small glass of orange juice, Matt orders oatmeal with extra butter and a large orange juice and Lute orders bacon, two fried eggs "up", rye toast, "no jelly, please." He likes to put salt and pepper on his rye toast. Some think it strange-he doesn't care, it tastes good to him-and a large orange juice.

As the waitress departs, Setaan asks, "Well, what did you think of last night?"

Lute replies, "That was most bizarre event I have ever witnessed."

"Me too. That was really something. You know Setaan," Matt stammers, "the Geist Essers were chanting Anima. That is the word that we heard gasping out from that dying man all those years ago. What is the connection?"

She replies, "That is jumping the gun a bit. I would rather tell the tale in a more logical fashion. I believe that I will be able to fill in the details better that way."

Matt and Lute nod assentingly.

Setaan continues, "Geist Essers or Soul Eaters are found all over God's green earth, on all continents, on the islands, in big and small communities. Where there are no Geist Essers in parts of the world they are sent to those locations when needed."

Lute interrupts, "Sent? How? Why? By whom?"

Setaan allows the interruption and answers. "Seele Fresser is the leader."

She holds up her hand to ward off another interruption from Lute.

She continues. "Seele Fresser is the one in charge of the Geist Essers. He was the leader whom you saw last night directing the proceedings in THE CHURCH FOR SOULS. He travels the world leading the various churches during the rituals, as you witnessed last night.

It is not known how he knows where to go when. Nor do we know how he gets to each location. He just seems to appear where a church service is taking place at the midnight hour. At the first strike of midnight the ritual begins.

I received an email from Seele Fresser. I used to get a letter postmarked Rome, Italy telling when we are to begin harvesting souls and when the reaping service will begin. The reaping service is what we call the processional with stainless bowls filled with the souls that we have harvested."

"What about the word Anima that is heard as people give their last breath?" asks Lute.

"That is the response from the mind realizing that it no longer has a soul. It is a sort of cry of despair, a kind of calling out in anguish.

I have a feeling that you two may have seen that dead, empty look on a few people. When we take people's souls, the outward sign of the loss is the empty dead look in their eyes. It does not last long, though. After a very short time their outward expression returns to what it was before the harvesting."

"And before you ask, no we had nothing to do with Digger's death. We were trying to get to him to let him know what we are doing and to tell him that what we are doing is as it is supposed to be."

Setaan continues her story about Digger saying, "What happened to Digger is that he had driven out to the park and parked his car at the lookout point. You know the place where you can see the ocean?" "Suddenly, a group of biker skinheads came down the road from up north. They surrounded Digger in his car and began beating on the car with bats. Digger gathered his wits about him and tore out of there in a cloud of dust. The bikers followed."

"All this happened so fast that the Geist Essers in the van was taken by surprise and did not react fast enough to do anything but follow."

"They saw the whole thing. The bikers easily caught up to him and began pummeling the car. Digger, in desperation, took that corner way too fast, the tire blew and he went flying into the tree. There was nothing our people could do."

"We had been in constant radio contact with the van and instructed them to stay as at far enough distance that they could observe but not be seen."

"They left when Luther here showed up."

"By the way, we did not eat his soul. In fact, we were not permitted to. We were told not to. I mean, Seele Fresser told us not to eat his soul."

Lute gave out a quiet prayer, "Thank you, Father."

"I don't know from whom he got that order. He specifically told us not to."

Seele Fresser, our leader, tells us which souls to take. I do not know exactly who tells him or how he is told; but I have my ideas-"

Lute breaks in with, "What ideas? Who?"

Setaan relies. "What I was going to say is that I will not be telling you that either. I do not know, therefore, I should not be telling stories out of school."

"That sounds like a wise adage to follow in this case," Matt chimes in.

Matt had one more question, "Why are you telling us all this?"

"Well, Seele Fresser told me to. He told me to invite you to the Reaping ritual. He wanted you to see it. I do not know why. Remember, we were looking to tell Digger about us before he met his demise."

Lute is about to ask another question when Setaan cuts him off. "No more, boys. Seele Fresser told me to tell you all that I have said and to say no more."

The breakfasts had been brought to them during their conversation. They barely noticed it happening. They even ate without much awareness either.

Setaan finishes off her coffee, wipes her mouth with the paper napkin, stands (the boys stand), shakes each of their hands, thanks them for their time and consideration and says, "Seele Fresser wants to see you tonight."

Both nod their heads while Lute includes, "What time?"

"Eleven thirty tonight, if you would like, at the church."

Matt says, "We will be there with bells on. Thank you, Setaan. Thank you very much."

"Oh wait," Setaan abruptly says before she forgets. "There is one more thing that you need to know. I was the Geist Esser who harvested that man's soul; the soul of the man whom you three boys found."

Matt's and Lute's mouths drop open a little bit and their eyes get a bit bigger. They just stare at her. It never occurred to them that she had been the Geist Esser to have done that to him. Well, it had to be someone, so it might as well have been her.

"He was a very bad man. He tried to do nasty things to me at the tracks. Instead of him doing his nasty deeds, I took his soul. He must have known something was happening to him because he went screaming out of my car."

"The last I saw of him he was tearing his way through the brush next to the tracks. I am guessing that he fell down the embankment and gashed his head and knocked himself out. That was when you boys found him."

"Well, you know the rest."

Matt says, "We heard the man gasp out Anima as he died. None of us has forgotten that. That has affected our lives. It is a relief to know what it was that we heard."

She shakes hand with them and says, "Adieu. I will not be seeing you again."

Setaan smiles and walks out of Jerry's Diner.

Matt and Lute sit back down into the opposite sides of the booth. Lute sits in Setaan's seat to finish off the French toast and the remaining piece of crispy bacon.

Matt is sipping his coffee, enjoying it. Jerry's has the absolute best coffee in town. He wishes that this type of coffee was available for home use. Too bad.

It's like standing rib roast. Try as one will, a home-cooked prime rib roast does not even come close to the yumminess that is gotten at a good steakhouse. Why is that?

It is said that if one were to coat the outside of the meat with olive oil the meat's taste hints at the restaurant's magnificent flavor.

Matt says, "Lute, we may be becoming privy to information that has been hidden from the world for who knows how long, maybe forever. We will find out tonight.

Lute leaves the tip while Matt pays the check. They both go outside into a most gorgeous day. Everything looks cheerful and happy. Maybe because that is way they are thinking.

Their plan for the day is sleep. Then wake up about five, have dinner and make ready for eleven thirty at the church.

CHAPTER TWENTY TWO

After having slept until five in the evening, awakened and supped on a chuck roast, potatoes, carrots, onions and a few other vegetables that Lute had put into the crock pot when they returned from Jerry's earlier that morning, they sat in the living room ruminating on the last few day's happenings.

They talked about the dead eyes that had been seen on people. Now they know that their souls had been harvested right then and there in broad daylight. And it was done by ordinary looking people.

What they did not completely understand was how the people were picked and what actually caused it to happen.

They had gone into the creepy THE CHURCH FOR SOULS and had seen bizarre things; bizarre beyond belief. They actually saw robed people young and old, at least two hundred of them, processioning down an aisle, holding with both arms, large stainless steel bowls filled with greyish, creamy-colored highly viscous liquid that was said to be souls. During the processional these Geist Essers are chanting an archaic word for souls, Anima. When they reach the front of the church they slowly pour their ooze into a large hole fashioned into an altar of some sort. As they dump they say the word Anima.

They think they know that this rite has restarted about three years ago when THE CHURCH FOR SOULS was rebuilt and Setaan returned to town.

They also realize that each of the two hundred Geist Essers carried nearly full stainless steel bowls. That means a lot of souls. A whole lot of souls.

After this discussion, Matt picks up Lute's laptop and Lute grabs a beer and goes to his easel to paint. They have a few hours to kill before they leave for the appointed rendezvous with Seele Fresser at THE CHURCH OF SOULS.

Matt realizes that they do not know what Seele Fresser means. He types in German to English translator. He types in Seele Fresser. The German to English translation is SOUL EATER. Creepy Matt calls out, "Hey, Lute. Do you want to hear something creepy?"

"I would rather not."

"Seele Fresser translates to SOUL EATER. How is that for creepy? We have Geist Esser or Spirit or Ghost Eater and the leader is Seele Fresser or Soul Eater. There are two types of soul eaters; two different purposes. Geist Essers harvest souls; Seele Fresser eats them. I wonder if he actually eats them or if the eating is when they are dumped into the hole.

I will make a list of questions that I will try to ask, if we are even allowed to ask questions. You keep on doing what you are doing. I have this one. I will say the questions out loud. You change it if you think necessary and add your own when the spirit hits you. Pun intended.

I am going to list them out as they come to me; no apparent order."

Matt does some searching for "Word" and the Verdana font that he likes so much. It has a good clear look about it, the spacing is good, it is very readable, and the size is ideal for aging eyes.

Matt types and says out loud the following list of questions for Seele Fresser:

- How does souls harvesting work
- Why is harvesting souls done
- Why is it done; need a better understanding

- What is that dump hole in the front of the church in the altar
- How long has harvesting been going on
- How many people know about this
- Why does it not matter that is being told to us know

Lute chimes in, "I have been wondering about the temperature of the stainless steel bowls. Stainless is cool at room temperature. Maybe the ooze is also."

- Why has the harvesting been an apparent secret
- Is the pace of the harvesting changing

Matt will type up the list when they finish and take it along with them tonight.

CHAPTER TWENTY THREE

It is a beautiful full moon sky overhead as they speed along the roadway to THE CHURCH FOR SOULS. There is not much traffic at this hour and as Lute pulls into Dam Lane and turns around the bend to the church, Matt says, "Look there is only one car. Is that not the one that Seele Fresser came in last evening? It is, I am sure of it."

Lute nods absently. He is engrossed in the appearance of the black church with the shiny red doors. The torches surrounding the building are lighted and are making a vibrant, eerie, flickering sight. Creepy.

They are right on time, 11:30 p.m.

As Lute pulls up to park, Seele Fresser appears from around the right side of the building. He walks up the car and opens Lute's door and welcomes them out of the car.

They both exit the car and close the doors. Matt walks around to where Lute and Seele Fresser are standing. The size of Seele Fresser is even more impressive, they notice now that they are closer to him than they had been last evening. He is wearing a light grey, very expensive suit; not a rumple in the shoulders and the lapels lay flat. His shoes are shiny and his tie is dark blue, making his white shirt stand out.

Seele Fresser extends his hand to Matthew and Luther and warmly greeting them and beckons them to come into the church. The boys hesitate. This is not a normal, everyday run of the mill kind of meeting with a "normal" type person. Yes, it is a bit scary as Lute will remark to Matt when they return home early the next morning.

The torches are flickering away, making the church building seem to dance.

Matthew steps forward. Luther follows suit. They follow Seele Fresser into THE CHURCH FOR SOULS.

The enormity and the building and the fire fed dancing windows is awe inspiring. They seem more vivid tonight than last night; the colors are fantastic, and the dancing movements are incredible. Maybe this is because they are the only ones in the here and their vision is not impeded by heads and shoulders of the Geist Essers. Also, the room looks larger now that there are not two hundred plus people there.

The three stand in place, engulfed in the spectacle.

The three stand facing each other, Seele Fresser's face is now seen in entirety. He has high cheek bones enclosing a perfectly shaped nose. His eye brows are perfectly shaped as if they had just been shaped by a professional. His lips are full; both upper and lower. But it is the eyes that make this man the perfect looking specimen of mankind. They are cat blue, a beautiful Caribbean ocean cay blue. In short, this man was the most handsome man either of them had ever seen and probably never would again.

Matthew breaks the trance, "Thank you for the invitation to come here this evening. It is certainly unexpected."

Luther breaks in, "And thanks for last night. It was quite interesting."

Matthew says, "Luther and I have learned quite a lot these past few days, to say the least. What you all are doing seems very frightening on the surface. But the fact that you have shown us all that you have and allowed Setaan to meet with us at breakfast, as well as telling us last night about the things that you do seems to make what you are doing less creepy.

You have invited us out here for a reason that we can only guess at. We assume that you are going to tell us more about what is going on here and elsewhere and will maybe let ask questions. We have a whole list of them."

Seele Fresser smiles, nods and says, "Do not fear. Yes to both. I am here to let the two of you know what the Geist Essers and I are all about. What you do with this information is up to you, but I must say that what I am about to impart is very serious and obviously very important to you and the rest of the world.

"Please do excuse me if I repeat a thing or two of what Setaan has already told you. I do so for emphasis."

Luther asks, "Why us? I mean, with all the people in the whole world Matthew Thomas and Luther St. Johns were chosen to receive this information."

"It is not I who has made this decision. I too receive my instructions from someone else. Setaan, now, gets her instructions from me via email. I get mine from another source via another method. It comes to me as a thought instructing me on what to do with whom, when and how.

For instance, this church, THE CHURCH FOR SOULS was rebuilt because a thought I had instructed me to do so. We began harvesting souls again based on a thought that I had. This is the way it has been for as long as I have been The Seele Fresser."

"You mean that you have not always held this position; that it is an appointed post?" Matthew asks.

"It is more of a destined position. I became a Geist Esser first. I didn't seek it, the opportunity just came to me and I became one. Actually, I do not believe I had a choice. It is sort of like being predestined to it. I cannot explain it better than that at this meeting. There just is not enough time here this evening."

Luther asks, "How many Geist Essers are there? If there are two hundred here-hold it a sec. I have the sense that Geist Essers are everywhere in the world. That means that there are millions."

"Yes. That is correct. There are Geist Essers everywhere. And where more are needed they move to the different areas where they can help with the harvesting. Setaan has moved a few times. She moved from here soon after you boys found that man by the tracks.

And I do believe that you have actually seen a few of them. You should have noticed that they look like everyone else in this world. That is because they are like everyone else. They are no different from the two of you. And that is because they are as one hundred percent human as the next man. We look the same, act the same, move the same, talk the same, eat, sleep, and do everything the same as the next man. There is nothing to distinguish us from anyone else. This is one reason that we have been doing what we do undetected since 1963.

"Setaan told you a little about harvesting. I will fill some of the gaps, but not quite yet. I want to take you into the basement for that.

I believe, right now, it is a good time to show you the dump hole in the altar."

As they walk toward the altar, Matt and Lute look at the dancing windows. The fire and graveyard windows are the most lively and eerie of the four. However, the other two are fantastic, also.

They follow Seele Fresser up the three steps and stand in front of the altar with the gaping hole in the center of it. It is spotless clean on the surface and down the black metal looking sides of the hole.

"This is called the Dump Hole. It is not a glamorous or fancy name. It is a functional name. This is where we dump the souls which have been harvested. The souls are carried down the aisles and dumped."

Luther asks his question, "What is the temperature of the souls? I would think that souls within the body would be at body temperature if indeed a spirt can have a temperature. But watching the Geist Essers holding those stainless steel bowls made me think that they were at room temperature."

"Interesting observation; yes and no."

Luther simply looks at him with a small, inquisitive smile.

"You are correct that the bowls are room temperature, therefore they feel cool to the touch. And the souls do not have a temperature. They are spirit, therefore is without temperature."

"Thank you."

"You're welcome."

The windows are still dancing the fire dance from the outside torches. The sconces and the chandelier are not lit.

Luther asks, "How does harvesting work? I mean, one moment a person has a soul, the next moment it is gone. How is it done?"

"We suck them out. It is like using a straw or a vacuum cleaner. We just pull them out and hold them within us until we can deposit them into the stainless steel bowls. There are lids that cover the bowls that stay on until the Dumping ritual.

"The how of it you will not understand. It is spiritual. I cannot explain it to you"

Matthew said, 'Yes, we can understand the complicated nature of it. I believe it not so important, the how of it."

"How do you choose which souls to eat?" Lute asks.

"Ah. That is the most important question. It goes to the core of life and existence; the purpose of living and the reason for dying."

He continues, "People have souls. You, me, everybody. It is the 'who we are' part our being. Our soul gives us our connection to each other and God."

"Some people truly get it when they hear 'the purpose of life is to love God with all you heart and all your soul.' They get it and they do it.

"Most of us do not understand; and I do mean most people."

Seele Fresser says, "We are not wanting for souls. We get almost all of them as it is. It does not really matter that people know. They have already been told of the penalty of sin."

"You see, it is our job here on earth to collect these souls. It is part of the way of the world. They say that it has been our job since the beginning."

Matthew comments to Lute, "Let me give you an analytical explanation of what Seele Fresser has spartanly said."

"We need to go back to the beginning; the beginning of the world. No, let's go back before the beginning."

"Before there was a universe God had created the spirit realm; the angels. There, angels were designed to sing the praises of God. Lucifer was one of these angels, he is described as a beautiful angel.

"Angels apparently have pride because Lucifer desired to be like God. He felt that he should not be second to God. He wanted even footing with the Godhead."

Lucifer rebelled and took as many as one third of all the angels with him out of heaven."

"Now comes the beginning. God created the world and all that is in it and on it and in the air. He created man and woman. He looked at His creation and called it good. God created everything for his loving pleasure."

"Adam and Eve, the two whom God created, were given the Garden of Eden to dwell in. They walked and talked with God."

"Then tragedy struck. That angel who rebelled is in the Garden of Eden and causes Adam and Eve to sin.

"Adam and Eve are banished from the Garden, never to return."

"Now Luther, you need to understand that what may seem as random incidences were fully foreknown by God. He allowed the Luciferic rebellion. He allowed Adam and Eve to learn the knowledge of Good and Evil."

"Luther, do you remember the story of Job?"

"Yes," Luther replies. Seele Fresser, who has been listening, unnecessarily nods.

"As a brief refresher, in a nut shell, Satan, Lucifer, asks God if he may be allowed to disrupt Job's life into hatred toward God. God allows it. Satan fails. God lets bad things into the world. He does not cause them, He allows them.

"God is sovereign. God is omniscient. He is love. He allows the world to unfold as it does; a natural evolution.

"God has already declared the world good, even with Lucifer in it. God has a plan for everyone. Everyone is where they are supposed to be at any given time, day or night. Everyone is doing what they are doing because God has it planned this way.

"In other words, everything is right with the world."

Luther nods understandingly and says, "God could have decided to collect the souls any way He wanted to. He chose the Geist Essers."

Matthew exclaims, "Ah! I now understand what it is saying all through the Bible. You remember the 23 Psalm? Right?"

Luther says, "Yes. I remember that one pretty well."

"Remember the part that says, '...Give us this day our daily bread...' And remember **Matthew 6:25-34**" For this reason I say to you, do not be worried about your life, as to what you will eat or what you will drink; nor for your body, as to what you will put on. Is not life more than food and the body more than clothing? Look at the birds of the air, that they do not sow, nor reap nor gather into barns, and yet your heavenly Father feeds them. Are you not worth much more than they? And who of you by being worried can add a single hour to his life?

"This passage tells us that we do not need to be anxious. Everything is in God's loving hands. Everything is fine."

There is a pause. Luther is absorbing all that has been said.

Luther asks, "That group that burned your church. They called you Evils, why."

Seele Fresser replies, "Those who will retain their souls, those who trust God and Jesus, can see that what one says Evils is likely one who will lose his soul.

"Follow me; I want to show you something."

They head to the back of the church, Seele Fresser lights a candle held in a copper candle holder and they head down the stairs with Seele Fresser leading the trio into the basement.

While descending the stairs, Luther asks, "How do you get from one place to another?"

"That is another one of those questions that I am unable to describe to you. Just take it that I do get from place to place rather quickly."

When they reach the bottom of the stairs, Seele Fresser begins lighting three candled sconces running down the walls. He starts with the back wall working his way along the right wall. As each sconce is lit a mural is exposed. The picture is a collage of people, some just faces, and others fully formed. The mural is from floor to ceiling. As Seele Fresser reaches the front wall, there is enough light to show that the left wall is blank. It has no pictures.

Luther exclaims as he nears the end of the finished part of the collage saying, "Hey Matthew, we know her. It is Janey. Seele Fresser, what is going on? Janey is such a nice girl. Why is her soul taken?"

Seele Fresser immediately says, We obey what Our Father says for us to do. We do not judge. Remember, it is not how good you are, how nice you are, or how well you keep the commandments; it is whether you are predestined for heaven. And that is all I am going to say on this subject. Matthew can explain this to when you get home.

"You probably notice quite a few people whom you know. I am certain that some of them will be quite a surprise to you."

Matthew says, "We always figured that our souls left when we die."

"They always have and still do, but some now are harvested. Something has changed. And the "why" of harvesting souls I cannot tell you. I do not know."

"There is no way that we can take the soul of a believer in God. We can only take souls of non-believers. These non-believers are the ones who break the Commandments of God; The Ten Commandments and the other tenants which God has declared."

"The breaking of God's Law is the giving away of your soul. It's as simple as that."

"That is a sort of reminder to them of what they have done to their lives. They went against God's Law and rules. The penalty is death. And death comes to them because they gave away their souls willingly. They lived unredeemed lives," Seele Fresser said.

"In other words, these people give us their souls. They basically throw them away."

Matthew and Luther are stunned. The people actually give away their souls willingly.

Luther says, "Oh my God. Major creepy."

Matthew asks, "Do you still have your soul?"

Seele Fresser does not answer immediately, almost as if deciding whether to respond or not. He must have decided ti tell them because he says, "No. I do not have a soul."

Matthew says, "I am so very sorry to hear that."

Seele Fresser smiles and says, "It is alright. This is the way God has set up the world. I have never had a soul."

"What?" gasps Matthew and Luther, together.

"No and it is the way it should be. For you see, I am an angel; God's servant. We have no souls."

"You are? You look just like any of the other people in the world," Luther pleads.

"That is right. The spirit world is different from your material, physical world. Remember in the Bible when different people are met by angels? We angels can do that. This is one of our attributes."

"So the wise man will consider the possibility that any one he meets is potential angel. We are here to assist you. Help you along your path to heaven."

Matthew asks, "You said earlier that you started harvesting souls in 1963. Why then has the harvesting accelerated; as if something is coming soon?"

"I cannot answer that. What happens will happen as God has planned; not before and not after. In His time."

Luther asks, "Why has it been secret? I assume is has been."

"Yes it has been secret until now. You and Matthew are the first to know about this."

"Why Luther and I, why now…," asks Matthew?

"I believe you know the answer to that. It is basic theology," interrupts Seele Fresser.

As they leave THE CHURCH FOR SOULS they shake Seele Fresser's hand, thank him and they head toward Luther's car. They both stop and look up. The stars in the sky are shining. The trees are gently swaying. They feel at peace. They know that all is right with the world. It is in good hands; the hands of God.

EPILOGUE

It is 10:30 in the morning. He usually awakens at 6:00. But since they stayed up so late last evening, sleeping late is expected. They have both been burning the candle at both ends for the many days that Matt has been in town so, the rejuvenating sleep is a welcome relief.

He rolls out of bed and pads his way to the bathroom. As he leaves his bedroom, he is overwhelmed with the wonderful smell of frying bacon. He loves the taste of bacon; he actually loves everything about bacon. Sometimes soft cooked bacon is best; as when eating with eggs, toast and coffee, or eaten by itself. Hard-cooked is best for bacon, lettuce and tomato sandwiches-a bite will snap off at the bite point instead of pulling the entire strip out from between the bread halves.

He manages to make it to the bathroom without heading to the kitchen and grabbing a slice of bacon. He brushes his teeth. He likes cleaning his teeth first thing in the morning. For him a fresh mouth is the best start to any day.

After brushing, he shaves; doing so because, for him, a hairy face makes it seem as if a man is hiding from the whole world. He likes to face the world head on.

Showering is next. He usually showers in the evening, before supper. He says that a clean body at night is the logical decision for two reasons. The first reason is the cleaned out pores of his body allow for the expelling of body heat easier than clogged pores. This allows for a more even body temperature while sleeping. The second reason is economical. The cleaner the sleeping body is the cleaner the sheets stay. Therefore the sheets need changing less often thus saving on water, detergent, dryer sheets and electricity for the washer and drier. And since he lives alone he is the one who does the laundry.

As he walks through the living room, Lute calls out from the kitchen asking, "How do you want your eggs?"

"Two of them. Up."

Matt enters the kitchen, the sun is streaming through windows, the bringing the room to life with a bright glow.

Lute is at the stove cracking the last two of four eggs into the frying pan. A stack of buckwheat pancakes is on the table in the nook along with glasses of orange juice, plates, utensils, butter, napkins and a very worthwhile bottle of maple syrup.

Matt has not had buckwheat pancakes since he was in high school. They were a favorite of his father, so every now and then Mom would give him a treat and not do the cooking, allowing dad to make his favorite pancakes for Saturday morning breakfast. They have a wonderful aroma and flavor that is mouth-watering. With buttery maple syrup there is likely not a better breakfast to be set before a king.

Lute delivers the eggs to the table, placing two of the eggs on top of the already buttered three-tiered stack. Matt calls this two on three.

They eat in relative silence, due to the incredible events of yesterday. They are each mulling over what they were told by Seele Fresser; the incredible fact that people are giving their souls to Geist Essers, willingly, and that this has been going on all over the world since Adam and Eve left the Garden of Eden. As well as Geist Essers and Seele Fresser being angels, and that the rate of soul eating is increasing all over the world, thus making one think that something is very soon going to happen to mankind.

Oh, and yes, the buckwheat pancakes are yummy.

After they wash the few dishes, dry them and put them away, Lute drives them to the center of town where they park in the downtown park's parking lot.

They exit the car and mosey over to a white-painted, metal park bench and sit.

Lute looks up at the deep Colorado blue sky. It is cloudless. It is a beautiful seventy three degree late morning with a gentle breeze. Perfect.

"Lute, we were told that the Geist Essers will take people's souls anywhere at any time. That means that it occurs when people are walking, standing, sitting, eating, running, drinking, reading, sleeping, while at church, at work, at home; anywhere at any time.

"We know that the people's eyes become momentarily blank at the time of the taking.

"And the Geist Essers can and do look like any full blooded human being. They dress up. They dress down. They dress casual. They dress sporty. They dress the same way as all of us, there is no difference. Geist Essers look just like us.

"I wonder if we can see more soul-takings."

Lute relies, "You mean go around looking for Geist Essers sucking souls out of people? Huh. That sounds like a great adventure. Let's do it!"

And so it begins.

They look around at all the people in the park.

Lute remarks, "There has to be nearness between the Geist Essers and the soul givers; knowing this will aid in our quest. Proximity is the key.

"Yes. We are going to have to see each of their faces at the same time when they meet up, because we do not know which is taking and which is giving," replies Matt.

They realize that they are going to have to move around a lot. They are going to have to pick and choose their prey carefully. They will need to split up.

It is good that God allowed man to invent smart phones; they are going to come in handy. By using their phones, they can coordinate their quarry search. By using the camera feature, they can have video evidence of the transferences, if they see any at all.

Not only do they see and record one, they record many, dozens. They realize that so many souls were being given away. It appears that more people are giving them to Geist Essers than are keeping their souls. It could be, though, that they may have had their souls eaten at an earlier date. Regardless, more are losing their souls than keeping them.

Their recordings show people passing each other both face to face, overtaking, passing a seated person and so forth. Each video showed and inhalation from the Geist Esser and the blanking of the eyes in the other's face which lasted for a moment.

They returned to their staring white bench and view the videos. "It is amazing," Lute remarks, "at how many people are giving away their souls. Don't they understand that their soul is not coming back to them? It is gone forever; down the stainless pit in the many CHUCHES FOR SOULS around the world.

"Matt says, "Some know. Some do not. Some do not care. Some cannot help themselves. Some do not believe in a soul.

"Those who do care keep their soul because they have faith that Jesus is exactly who He says He is; the Son of God, God on earth. He died so that we can keep our soul, go to heaven and receive a new body and live in the presence of God for all of eternity. The others will not. They will be separated from the Godhead forever in hell.

Praise be to God.

Amen.

The End

CPSIA information can be obtained
at www.ICGtesting.com
Printed in the USA
LVHW031508091218
599826LV00002B/245/P